Angeline

By

Caroline Clemmons

Angeline
Bride Brigade 2
Caroline Clemmons

ISBN 978-1530413799

Copyright 2016 and 2022 Caroline Clemmons

Cover © Charlene Raddon, https://silversagebookcovers.com

Table of Contents

Chapter One

St. Louis, Missouri
April, 1873

Could she jump? Angeline Chandler set down her two cases and stared at the railroad tracks below the station platform. She gauged the approaching train's speed to determine how much time she had to decide. Tears running down her face, she considered the alternatives.

Turned out of her own home, sent away with only twenty dollars to her name and that now dwindled, what chance did she have to survive? How could she provide for the child growing inside her? Would she even survive on her own until time for the baby's birth?

A quick end seemed a preferable alternative to starvation. Suicide went against all she believed. She especially couldn't kill her own baby. Surely another situation would present itself, but she had no idea what it would be. But what? When?

A firm hand grabbed her arm. Angeline startled and looked into the face of a beautiful, dark-haired woman not much older than herself.

The other woman's lovely gray eyes filled with compassion. "If you don't have other plans, perhaps you'd care to accompany my friend, six young women, and myself to Texas. Why don't we step over to that bench and I'll explain." Without releasing her grip, she picked up one of Angeline's cases with her free hand.

Numb, Angeline carried the other suitcase and let herself be led like a child to the bench where a middle-aged woman joined them. The three sat down with her two cases by their feet. Angeline pulled her handkerchief from her sleeve and blotted her tears.

The lovely woman smiled. "My name is Lydia Harrison and this is my friend, Sophie Gaston. We're returning to our home in Tarnation, Texas a few hours southwest of Fort Worth. I've recruited six young women to come with us because there are no marriage-age women in our small town. Young men are moving to cities so they can find a wife and have a family."

The one called Sophie nodded. "My own son is one of those talking about leaving. I prevailed on Lydia to do something to keep the young men in Tarnation." With a wry smile, she sent Lydia a glance. "To repay me, she insisted I travel with her."

Lydia took Angeline's hand. "Perhaps you'd like to come with us, at my expense, of course. I have a large home where all the girls will stay until they've found the man they wish to marry. With so many men looking for wives, I don't expect they'll be with me long, but they're welcome to remain as long as they wish."

Angeline couldn't believe her ears. "Y-You're inviting *me* to come with you?" Was this too good to be true? She didn't want to end up in a brothel.

"Yes. The other six girls have gone walking around but I'm sure you'll like them. We're traveling in a private car because we began in Richmond and are going to Fort Worth."

Lydia gave a slight grimace. "I'm afraid from there we'll be forced to ride the stage, so the final part of the trip will not be easy or pleasant. Arriving home will be worthwhile, though. I love our little town."

"I doubt anyone will want to marry me." Who'd want to marry a woman carrying another man's child? Should she confess or keep her own counsel lest she ruin her opportunity?

Lydia waved at someone. "Here are the other girls now. I know it's a hurried decision, but we leave very soon and must board our car now."

Angeline hardly needed to contemplate. She'd prayed for a solution—surely this must be Divine intervention. "If you're sure, I'd love to accompany you to…what was the place in Texas?"

"Tarnation. A term my late husband used frequently, which inadvertently caused the town's name. I'll tell you all about the place during our trip." She made brief introductions and they boarded.

Angeline had traveled with her family to elaborate locales, but even her parents considered the new Pullman car luxurious. She had no idea such sumptuous private train service as this was available. The walnut paneling and crystal light fixtures were as impressive as any opulent hotel she'd visited.

Small silver and crystal vases attached between windows held fresh flowers. Thick white damask covered each of two dining tables at one side. The same side held thickly padded armchairs. On the other, eight bunks lined the wall—four on top and four on bottom. Oh dear, she wondered where she would sleep. No matter, she was lucky to be alive and would sleep on the thickly carpeted floor if necessary.

Lydia spoke to the porter, who soon returned with fresh linens and a pillow and showed them how to turn a chair into a bed. Since evening was near, he made up the bed for her. She sank onto it gratefully.

Lydia rubbed her hands together and swayed as the train moved. "Now we're all set. The porter will bring our supper in a few minutes. Angeline, I'm sure you're familiar with train travel and know the facilities are in the tiny room at the end of the car."

"I've ridden the train many times, but never in a private car. This is definitely a magnificent way to travel."

No one questioned why she'd joined them. Throughout their meal, the other girls chattered and appeared welcoming without prying. For a while, Angeline drifted on the relief of having a place to sleep and the first food she'd eaten in more than a day. She allowed herself to relax. No matter what happened later, for now she was fed and safe.

***

Angeline stepped off the stage and peered around. She wasn't sure what she anticipated, but this small, dusty town didn't fulfill her expectations. Businesses Lydia had described were there, but they had wooden fronts instead of brick. For now, she was too tired from the journey to care about them. Or to think about the group of masculine specimens who'd met the stage.

"Ladies, this way." Lydia led them like a pied piper, with a line of men following carrying their luggage.

Rachel said, "Imagine a home like that here in the middle of nowhere. Why, it looks like it belongs on a Virginia plantation."

Cassandra carried a valise. "Doesn't it? Except there it would likely be painted white instead of gray. But isn't the appearance appealing with the wine shutters and door and white trim?"

Once they were inside, Lydia sweetly thanked the men for their efforts and shooed them outside with a promise, "You'll all receive an invitation to our Friday reception."

Angeline could hardly wait to lie down. The stage ride had almost defeated her. Only the girl named Ophelia appeared more affected by the trip than she was, but Ophelia's friend Josephine helped her. Angeline had no one.

She drew Cassandra as her roommate and they were shown to a room next to that of Ophelia and Josephine on the second floor.

Cassandra prowled their quarters investigating every nook and drawer. "This is a surprising house for the location, don't you agree?"

"I'm so tired I can't properly appreciate our surroundings." She unfastened her shoes and slipped from her travel suit. "I'm sure I'm carrying several pounds of dust, but I just want to lie down."

"Me, too. Lydia said we have time for a nap before supper."

"Every bone and muscle in my body aches. I could sleep for at least a week but even an hour or two will help." She turned back the cover and crawled into bed. Within seconds she was asleep.

Someone gently tugged at her shoulder. She opened her eyes to see Cassandra standing beside the bed.

"Angeline, wake up. We're supposed to go down for supper in thirty minutes."

She burrowed into her pillow. "Not hungry. Just want to sleep."

"Okay, I'll tell Lydia. I doubt you'll be the only no-show for the meal. I'll try to bring you something in case you're hungry later."

"Thanks." At least that's what she thought. She wasn't certain she actually spoke the words.

When she woke the next morning, she believed she could at least survive the day. She dressed in fresh clothes. "Cassandra, thank you for your thoughtfulness last night."

The other girl ate the cheese she'd brought from supper and tossed the roll into the waste bin. "You slept so soundly you never even moved."

"I imagine we were all tired. Riding on that middle seat was horrid, wasn't it? I'm glad we rotated so no one had to sit there all the way."

Cassandra gazed into the mirror and fluffed her hair. "Except Ophelia. Something must be wrong with her back because she doesn't wear a corset and never leans against anything."

"Not me, I leaned on anything handy. If it weren't for this dratted corset, I'd have dissolved by now."

Laughing, they went down for breakfast. Afterwards, Lydia called her into another room. Scared out of her wits, Angeline followed. Was she being tossed out? Did Lydia suspect?

Inside a masculine office, Lydia sat beside a massive desk and invited her to take a seat nearby. The room was decorated with military memorabilia. A portrait of a handsome older man had pride of place on the wall behind the desk.

Lydia gestured toward the portrait. "My late husband, William."

"He's a handsome man, but older than you." She shouldn't have mentioned that. Her nervousness made her blurt out inappropriate things.

"Twenty years, but the difference in our ages didn't matter to me. He was so strong and dynamic that he seemed larger than life. I don't know if I'll ever get over losing him."

"My condolences." Angeline couldn't think of what else to say.

"I didn't see you at supper last night so I wanted to reassure myself that you're going to be all right. Are you feeling better this morning?"

"Yes, thank you." Before Angeline could think, she blurted, "You knew I planned to jump, didn't you?"

"I thought that was your intent, but plainly you didn't want to and I don't believe you would have. Dear, I've wondered what possessed as intelligent and beautiful a woman as you to contemplate killing yourself."

Angeline sighed heavily and lowered her head. She couldn't bring herself to meet her hostess' eyes but she sneaked a glance through her eyelashes. "Y-You can guess, can't you?"

Lydia nodded. "But I wondered if you would tell me."

"I'm grateful for your help and I don't want you to think I'm a bad person." She raised her head to meet Lydia's gaze. "I-I was unofficially engaged to a man…Horace's father and mine were friends and my father approved the alliance. We hadn't announced our engagement but Horace told me we'd soon be married and where we'd live. We'd made lots of plans."

She clasped her hands to stop them trembling. How she hated talking about her stupidity. "One afternoon we went for a carriage ride in the countryside. He parked in some trees and forced himself on me... it was horrible. Afterward, he apologized but said all engaged couples had intimate relations."

Lydia's eyes held no hint of judgment. "How awful for you."

Angeline pulled her handkerchief from her sleeve cuff in a nervous gesture. "The next time we met was at a party and he was cool. He had the nerve to tell me he was finished with me and could never marry a woman who wasn't a virgin. I was shocked and horrified—and angry. The only reason I wasn't a virgin was because he'd assaulted me."

"What happened when you learned you were pregnant?"

The humiliation was almost too much to bear and again she couldn't face her hostess. "I sent him a note. He replied he owed me nothing and never wanted to see me again. He said if I made a claim against him, he had friends who would swear they'd had relations with me too."

Lydia gasped. "What a heartless cad. I'm glad you didn't marry a man of that caliber."

Twisting the handkerchief in her hands, she explained, "I learned from a friend that he left for Europe that very day for his two-year grand tour."

"But then you had to tell your parents alone."

Angeline nodded. "When…when I told my parents, my father grew livid. He threw twenty dollars at me and yelled as he told me to pack what things I could carry and get out. My mother sat crying and didn't even look at me."

"I'm so sorry they weren't more understanding. How long was that before I met you?"

She raised her head and met Lydia's gaze. "You mean before you saved me? Only four days. I'd come from Hannibal to see if my aunt would help me. Just like her brother, she sent me on my way. I'd been wandering around the station for thirty-six hours."

"My dear, you didn't even have a place to sleep? You must have been exhausted."

"I didn't know where to go or what to do. None of my friends would have been allowed to help me even if they'd known. Their parents would have shared my father's opinion. I had no other relatives to turn to. Until you rescued me, I was on my own."

Lydia leaned over to squeeze her hand. "I'm so sorry, dear. How far along are you?"

Tears pooled in Angeline's eyes and she dabbed with the

handkerchief. "Three months. I promise I would never marry a man without telling him, but who will want another's baby?"

"Stop worrying, dear, and believe things will work out. You seem to me to be a kind and loving woman. I'm glad you have no intention of deceiving a serious admirer. I asked you in here to reassure you that you can stay with me as long as you need to."

Hot tears flowed down her cheeks and she sobbed her relief. When she could finally speak again, she said, "I was afraid you were going to ask me to leave. You're the kindest person I've ever met. When you helped me, you saved two lives."

"Don't feel I'm singling you out. I'll speak privately with each of you girls. I've been thinking of which men might interest a particular girl. Can you cook?"

"Yes, I'd learned because I thought I was to be married. I learned many things from our family's cook but I also took a cooking course from a chef. I don't know much about cleaning, but I can learn."

"Cooking will go a long way toward making your home a happy one. That's why I'll ask you and the others to help around the house. I have a cleaning lady, but you need homemaking skills."

"Thank you, Lydia. I'll try hard to learn everything I can so I can take care of my home, wherever it is."

Lydia stood and held out her hand. "Dry your eyes now and smile for me. Let's join the others, shall we?"

Chapter Two

Lydia welcomed Adam to her study. He was such a good friend and confidante and she relied on his moral support more than she should.

"Come in, Adam, and have your usual seat. I'll ring for Mrs. Murphy."

He held up a hand. "No need. I just stopped by to see how things are going with your Bride Brigade. You seem...I don't know, maybe confused or upset. What's wrong?"

She waved aside his concern but before long she'd shared Angeline's dilemma. When she'd finished, she placed a hand at her throat. "What's come over me, Adam? You know I usually keep any secret to myself."

"This won't be secret long. If she wants to marry, she'd better choose soon. How about Elias at the saloon? Maybe he wouldn't mind a fallen woman since he has a couple of questionable doves working for him."

"Angeline hardly compares to saloon girls." She held up her hand. "I know, those girls probably have a similar story, but I can't worry about them until I find husbands for those staying here."

"I hope you're not going to make them a project too." He held up a hand and closed his eyes. "Aww, don't even tell me if you are. What are you doing about this Angeline?"

Lydia tapped her forefinger against her chin. She knew who would be perfect for the girl, but didn't yet know if the two would mesh. Nature would have to take over.

"She's very pretty, don't you agree?"

"They all are, but I'm not sure which one she is."

"Dark blond hair, about six inches over five feet, and her eyes are gray."

He smiled. "I'm partial to gray eyes but guess I didn't pay

close attention to them. Who're you matching her with?"

"I'm thinking."

Looking assured, he nodded. "Elias, right?"

She smiled at him. "We'll see. Now tell me how you've been, dear friend, and all that's happened while I was away."

Chapter Three

The next morning, nausea attacked Angeline in force and she barely made the chamber pot before the heaves began.

Cassandra poured water from the ewer into the bowl then wrung a cloth in the cool water. "Wash your face and hands with this then lay the cloth on your throat."

Angeline cleaned her face and hands and lay back on the bed. "I must have eaten something that didn't agree with me."

Cassandra put the lid on the chamber jar and slid it under the bed. When she stood, she put her hands on her hips. "I have a pretty good idea what didn't agree with you. How far along are you?"

Her eyes wide now, Angeline pleaded, "Please, don't say anything to anyone. I promise Lydia knows and I would never consent to marry a man unless I'd already told him of my condition."

"I won't tell anyone as long as that's true. Was Lydia mad at you?"

"She'd guessed when she asked me to join your group." Angeline explained about how desperate she'd been.

"Many parents would do the same thing, which is scandalous if you ask me. Even if you were disappointed in your child, she's still your child. And how could you cast out and not love your grandchild?"

Cassandra waved off her comment. "Well, talking solves nothing. You need to come down and nibble on toast and have some tea. That will help what's ailing you."

Angeline sat up but hesitated. "I'm afraid to. I'd hate to be sick at the table."

"Try at least. If you never come to breakfast, the others will wonder why. I wouldn't tell but people being what they are, they'll speculate."

"You're right, I'll go eat. I don't want to lie, but I also don't want anyone to guess." She forced herself to dress but left her thick blond hair flowing down her back."

After watching her dress, Cassandra asked, "How can you wear your corset so tight?"

"My clothes won't fit unless I do. Soon they won't fit at all." Then what would she do? Angeline wondered if the seams could be let out or the few dresses she had could be altered. Perhaps the mercantile had some fabric that would coordinate.

After breakfast, she felt slightly steadier. Perhaps Cassandra had been right. She excused herself to go to the mercantile and check the fabric available. She had two dollars left she'd been saving until she was so weak she required food. Now at least she didn't have to worry about meals.

The morning breeze cooled her and a few cottony clouds drifted in the brilliant blue skies. Fresh air further revived her and she enjoyed the two block walk. While she chose the material she would use, her energy ebbed. After making her purchase from a man she remembered from their arrival, she tried to make conversation while he wrapped her package.

The vigor which had been with her on her walk had completely disappeared. In its place a clammy, smothering sensation overwhelmed her. If only she could reach Lydia's she'd be safe. She hardly remembered taking her fabric and going out the door.

The world spun and she reached out her hand to steady herself but found only air. She gasped for breath, unable to breathe. Her knees turned to rubber and she felt herself sinking.

Firm hands clasped her upper arms. "Miss, may I help you?"

She looked into the kindest hazel eyes she'd ever seen. His blond hair barely showed under his hat. "I don't know what came over me. I suppose I'm still tired from my journey."

He looped her arm onto his. "I'm the local pastor, Grady McIntyre. Please allow me to escort you to the Harrison home."

"Thank you, I'm Angeline Chandler. Frankly, I can use a solid arm to lean on for the walk." She clasped his forearm as she would a stair banister. For a minister, he was muscular and appeared strong.

"You must be one of the young women who came with Lydia. I couldn't get away to greet your arrival but I understand there was quite a reception committee."

She forced a smile. After all, he was gallant enough to help her and deserved a friendly response. "I was awfully tired. I hardly remember anyone except the mercantile owner and the sheriff. Lydia made a point of greeting them."

"I remember that trip and imagine by then you only wanted a bath and a bed. That's a tiring ride."

"Deadly. I'm surprised my teeth didn't fall out with all the bumps and rattles."

"Don't understand how anyone's brave enough to leave town. Once I arrived, I vowed never to leave."

She grinned at his attempt to cheer her. "Me, too. Do you and your wife live by the church?"

His face sobered. "I live in the parsonage. My wife died just over a year ago. She never recovered from our son's birth. Our...my son is eighteen months old."

What a terrible faux pas. "I apologize for reminding you of your sorrow and offer my sincere condolences. I imagine being a minister and raising a son alone keeps you very busy."

He smiled again, which relieved her. "Extremely. Mrs. Gallagher keeps him when I'm away from home. He gives her a time, though, and I'm not sure how much longer she'll consent to stay with him."

"I'll bet he's adorable. I don't know her, but if she's older then perhaps keeping up with him is tiring. Are you going to attend Lydia Harrison's socials and look for your son a new mother?"

"No young woman would marry a minister with a small child. I think it best if I tend to the congregation."

"Oh, I think you're wrong about no one marrying a man with a child. Still, I suppose being the preacher means you have to walk a fine line."

His voice held censure. "Don't feel sorry for me, Miss Chandler. I enjoy time with congregation members and especially with my son."

"I'm sure you do." That must be a touchy subject. "What's your son's name and does he look like you?"

Pride and love glowed on his face. "Matthew looks like me but his eyes are more blue than hazel. He's walking now, which keeps Mrs. Gallagher on the run."

She admired him for showing his love for his son so openly. "He sounds delightful. Is he talking yet?"

"He says words and short sentences. I guess more like phrases."

"What are his favorite words?"

"Embarrassing to admit, but they're 'no' and 'mine'." The minister laughed. "We've had discussions about both of those."

"I used to play with my neighbor's children on occasion. They change so fast at that age. He's lucky you're willing to spend time with him."

He sent her a puzzled glance. "That's what parents do."

Surely he didn't believe that. "Not all of them."

They reached the steps to Lydia's and Angeline paused and turned to face the minister. "Here we are. Thank you for helping me. I genuinely appreciate your assistance."

He guided her to the door then tipped his hat. "Let me know if I can aid you in any way. Good day."

She opened the door and sighed that she was home, or the closest she had to one. If she could make her way up the stairs, she'd be able to unlace this blasted corset and lie down. All she had to do was put one foot in front of the other.

Cassandra spotted her and hurried toward her. "Oh, you're back. Let's go to our room and you can show me what you purchased." Leaning near, she said, "Lean on me. You look positively gray."

"Thank you. I'm about to drop." She didn't say another word until they were in their room. Plopping across the bed, she unbuttoned her velveteen jacket and silk blouse.

"Here, let me help. Sit up. I should never have let you go out laced up that tight." Cassandra helped her remove the corset and then let her lie back down. When Angeline's breathing returned to normal, she explained what had happened.

"Oh, he sounds nice. Thank goodness he helped you." The other woman picked up her package and untied the string. "Now let's see what you have to redo your clothes."

"Nothing matched exactly, so I tried for coordinating. I know the result will be terrible, but I don't know what else to do."

Cassandra unfolded the pieces of fabric. "This black velvet will work for the suit you had on today. You bought a lot of this gray foulard, so I suppose you plan to make a new dress. Good, the dark green will make a new top." She looked in the wrapping and held up two spools of thread and a packet of needles and pins. "There's no trim."

"I didn't dare spend the money. I only had a couple of dollars left. I can take trim from the green dress in the armoire. It's the smallest thing I have so I know I can't wear it now."

Cassandra examined Angeline's clothes. "We can use the skirt and it will go with the dark green for a blouse."

Her heartbeat quickened. "We? Are you saying you'll help me?"

The other girl tilted her head. "Why wouldn't I? You've been nice to me."

Tears threatened to pour from Angeline's eyes. "I don't know how to thank you. I've felt so alone. I appreciate so much you being willing to help me and not telling anyone of my...predicament."

"If you've recovered enough, take this seam out while I take the green dress apart. We'll have to hurry if you're going to have something to wear to the social on Friday."

They worked companionably for most of the day. By evening, Angeline had fashioned a new top of the dark green and the green skirt had been let out in a way that she could tie it at the side and accommodate future growth.

"What a relief wearing something that fits will be available. I won't have to wear that strangling corset now."

"I don't think they're good for the baby. How could they be good for anyone? Lydia said most women in Tarnation only wear a corset on Sundays, if even then."

"Wonderful. I can't tell you how happy that makes me." Angeline hung the new clothes in the armoire. She turned to regard the dress she'd worn this morning. "I'd better force myself back into that for this evening."

She laced up her corset over her chemise. How she hated the trapped feeling of not being able to take a deep breath. At least she had great posture.

Cassandra held up a blue dress. "You can use part of the drape on this to form a design and enlarge the top so no one can tell the difference."

Buttoning her blouse, Angeline glanced up. "You're very good at this. You could own a dress shop."

Cassandra help up both hands in mock surrender. "Not me. I

want to be a woman of leisure with servants to wait on me hand and foot."

"Then I hope that's what you get." They left the room to join the others.

The next morning, Angeline heaved into the chamber pot again. After she'd recovered and washed up, she dressed in her altered skirt and new blouse. "I intend to go thank the minister for his help. Maybe I can also talk to him about forgiveness for my situation."

Cassandra shrugged as if she thought Angeline wasted her time. "Might make you feel better. If I get bored, I'll work on the suit you had on yesterday. It's too nice not to wear. You'll need thread this color if you still have enough money to buy a spool as you pass the mercantile."

After breakfast, Angeline excused herself and walked toward the church. What if the minister had gone to call on members of his congregation? She supposed she could use the exercise even if he wasn't home.

She found the parsonage neatly painted white to echo the church. She knocked on the door.

Grady McIntyre answered, holding a squirming toddler. "Miss Chandler, may I help you?" He stepped aside to admit her.

She entered, curious about his home. "I came to thank you for helping me yesterday."

"Not necessary at all. This is Matthew. He's being a handful this morning." He set the boy on the floor.

Angeline knelt to the child's level. "Hello, Matthew."

The child reached for her and she picked him up. "What a lovely, strong boy you are."

The little boy grabbed for her hair, which she'd left partly down.

The minister took him from her. "He's liable to get your clothes dirty."

She didn't know how to approach the real reason she'd come so she blurted out the truth. "I wondered if I could talk to you."

"Of course. Have a seat. Mrs. Gallagher isn't here today, but I'll just put Matthew in the next room with his toys." He disappeared and was back quickly. "That doesn't guarantee he'll stay there, so we'd best get started."

"Do ministers keep things private like a priest or a lawyer?"

"You can be positive anything you tell me is kept in strict confidence. What's bothering you, Miss Chandler?"

"Do you believe God really forgives our mistakes if we're truly sorry?"

"I believe that with all my being. All that's necessary is that you ask His forgiveness with an earnest heart."

Angeline exhaled her relief and stood. "Thank you. I appreciate you seeing me without an appointment."

He rose and walked with her. "You don't need an appointment to see me. Please stop anytime. I'm always pleased to see a smiling face."

She wondered aloud, "Do you see many of the other kind?"

His grimace answered the question, but he said, "Not many, but those I see are enough to remain at the forefront of my memory longer than I wish."

Walking back to Lydia's, Angeline thought about Matthew and wondered what her baby would be like at that age. What would happen to her and her child? Would her baby even live to be a toddler? She made a promise that if a man asked her to marry him, as long as she believed he would never harm her child, she'd accept his proposal.

She supposed she still believed in love, but she doubted she would ever open herself to its pain again. Having failed so badly in deciphering Horace's character, how could she trust her judgment? Settling for security for her child would be enough.

She turned in at the store and went inside. After finding the correct thread, she took it to the counter.

An older woman was there, leaning on her cane. "Michael, how soon can you deliver that flour? I let myself run out and I can't make bread for my dinner without it. Found too many weevils to sift in what I had and tossed it in the rubbish."

The man she remembered was mayor said, "I'll get it to you as soon as I can. In the meantime, why don't you stop at the café and have a meal there? Do you good to eat someone else's cooking for a change."

The woman sagged on her cane. "No, I need to go home and put my feet up."

Angeline didn't know what prompted her to speak, other than the woman appeared to be in pain. "I could carry the flour for you, ma'am."

"Would you? Why that's kind of you. You must be one of the Bride Brigade girls."

Angeline frowned at the term. "Bride Brigade?"

The owner, Mr. Buchanan, shook his head. "That's what folks are calling the young women Lydia Harrison brought back with her."

She grinned. "Then I'm one of the Bride Brigade. My name is Angeline Chandler."

"I'm Keturah Eppes and I guess you've met our mayor, Michael Buchanan. I believe you should just say you're Angel, for you're one today."

"I'll be pleased to help you as soon as I pay for my thread."

She quickly handed over the money for her purchase and picked up the flour. She prayed she wouldn't have a fainting spell. Without her corset binding her, she felt much better today.

Michael handed her the thread. "Thank you, Miss Chandler. I appreciate you helping Mrs. Eppes. I'd have to close the store in order to make a delivery. Otherwise she'd have to wait until this evening."

After slipping the thread in her purse, she picked up the flour. "I'm pleased to get to know people in my new home. Shall we go, Mrs. Eppes?"

Angeline chatted with the elderly woman as they walked slowly toward Mrs. Eppes' home. The spring breeze refreshed her but the flour was growing heavy by the time they reached the widow's home three blocks away.

At the door, Mrs. Eppes turned to her. "You come in and let me make you a cup of tea. How lovely to learn a pretty young thing like you also is nice."

The offer sounded genuine and she could use refreshment. "I don't want to trouble you, Mrs. Eppes. Perhaps you'll sit down and let me make the tea."

A relieved smile split the woman's face. "What a grand idea if you don't mind. I could do with a rest. I'll just sit in my rocker and put my feet up a bit if you're sure you don't mind."

"You go right ahead. I'll bring your tea in as soon as it's brewed."

"There's milk in the ice box and sugar in the bowl and I take both. Jo Jo Greenberg just brought a new block of ice yesterday so the milk should be nice and cool."

Angeline wondered if she could find everything without

prying. She spotted the teapot on the kitchen table. With little trouble she found the cups and saucers. "Your home is spotless."

"Well, I do like things a certain way. Nowadays I have more trouble keeping them just so, though. Good thing Mrs. Querado comes in a half day once a week."

When the tea was ready, Angeline served Mrs. Eppes in the parlor of the small home. Sitting across from her hostess, she relaxed and enjoyed listening to the widow talk about her late husband and their life together. After taking the cups back to the kitchen and rinsing them out, she promised to return another day.

Chapter Four

Angeline arrived at Lydia's in time for dinner. She helped clean up after the meal then went to her room to work on the purple velvet suit. The only velveteen fabric the mercantile had was black. Analyzing the un-seamed suit, she'd planned a solution to alter the garment.

Cassandra came in. "Thought I'd see if you need any help. What took you so long?"

Angeline explained about Mrs. Eppes. "Now I'll work on this. Thank you for taking out the seams."

Her friend ran her fingers across the garment. "Love the feel of the fabric."

Angeline spread the black velvet on the bed and gauged her design before making a cut. "Everyone who's seen me wear the outfit will know it's had been enlarged."

"Not necessarily. Just don't volunteer any information."

Worry dogged her. "What can I say if someone asks? I hate to lie."

Cassandra tapped a finger against her lip. "Say you tore the fabric and hated to discard the suit so you reworked the design instead."

That lightened her mood. "I guess that's really what happened since the garment's been torn apart. I'm lucky you're my roommate, Cassandra."

"Think nothing of it. We're supposed to support and encourage one another, aren't we? This will be just as pretty when you're finished. You just have to remember to allow for growth."

Angeline paused and touched her expanding stomach. "Soon people will be able to tell. What will I do? Who'll want to marry me?"

Cassandra sent her a remonstrative glare. "Do you remember how many men met the stage? You're a beautiful woman. I think we all are, in fact. There are more men who want us for wives than there are women to go around."

She waved off her roommate's remark and resumed planning her alterations. "Wanting a wife is one thing, but accepting one who's carrying another man's child is quite different. Most men would prefer remaining single. And I could never marry a man unless I was sure he would be kind to my child."

"Angeline, Lydia promised she would only introduce us to men of that caliber. I believe her or I wouldn't be here."

She paused and allowed hope to seep into her heart. "You're right. Lydia did promise, didn't she? Okay, if a man proposes, I'll tell him about the baby. If he doesn't withdraw, then I'll accept."

"Okay, that's settled. Regardless of your condition, I suspect you'll have several men offer for you. Now, let's get your wardrobe, such as it is, in shape."

***

Grady McIntyre left Matthew with Mrs. Gallagher and went to call on the elderly and ill of his congregation. In front of the mercantile, he met Lydia Harrison. When she saw him, she sat on the bench in front of the store and patted the seat beside her.

Reluctantly, he joined her. He figured a lecture was on the way because he hadn't accepted her invitation to her reception to introduce her girls to eligible men.

Sure enough, her first words were, "Grady, why aren't you coming tonight?"

He exhaled the pain of his loneliness. "What's the point? You know how many men want to marry one of your Bride Brigade."

"Why would that discourage you? Have you no sense of adventure and competition? Matthew needs a mother. I don't think Mrs. Gallagher can keep up with him much longer."

"I agree Matthew needs a mother and also that he's about exceeded Mrs. Gallagher's energy. However, none of those beautiful young women would want to take on a man with a child when they have their pick of men."

Her gaze held sympathy. "Ridiculous. You at least owe yourself the opportunity to try. Come tonight, won't you?"

He shook his head and gazed at the distant hills. "I don't think so. Lydia, I appreciate what you're doing for the town. I hope this means there'll soon be weddings and then new life in Tarnation."

"That's my wish, too. But you're one of the nicest men in town and I hoped you'd find one of the girls to your liking."

He couldn't shake his dejection. "Thank you. Your saying so means a lot to me. I have to admit I've been doubting myself lately."

"Harlie Jackson and Ulys McGinnis still giving you a hard time, are they? Those two don't approve of anything. I doubt they really even like one another."

He grimaced, agreeing with Lydia. "McGinnis thinks whatever Jackson tells him and Jackson has made it his mission to get rid of me as minister. I don't know how long before he turns others against me."

She half-turned on the bench to face him. "Two people out of the town are not going to force you to leave. You keep being the good minister you are. And think about coming to meet the girls tonight."

"I met one, Miss Chandler. She almost fainted by where we're sitting and I walked her to your home. Seemed like a nice young woman."

"She is. Actually, each of them is suitable. Otherwise, I'd have found somewhere else for them. I brought home only women I'd want for neighbors."

"Good planning." He stood. "I'd better get over to check on Mrs. McAdams. She hasn't been feeling well. Nice to see you, Lydia."

He strode quickly toward the McAdams home before Lydia could try her hand at more persuasion. Heaven knew he wanted to meet a woman who would share his life and love Matthew and him. But, if she'd just love Matthew, he'd take her.

***

At the reception, Angeline lined up with the other girls to meet the men as they were presented. Several were really handsome, others passable, and all seemed nice. She glided around the room, talking to first one and then another.

Panic hit her. Already she could see couples forming, yet none of the men singled her out. Handsome Mr. Buchanan had honed in on Josephine right away, although Josephine didn't appear interested. What was wrong with that girl?

Lydia spent her time talking to the sheriff. Angeline thought there was something going on between those two, but maybe they were just friends. This evening, she'd met a doctor, ranchers, cowboys, a carpenter. She'd also met owners of the bank, the livery stable, the saloon and the opera house, the freight office, the mercantile, and the newspaper. There were more businesses in town, but she supposed their owners were already married or deemed unsuitable.

Adam Penders, the sheriff, made a blunt point of introducing her to Elias Kendrick, the owner of the saloon and opera house. Mr. Kendrick seemed nice, but apparently he didn't feel any more spark for her than she did for him. She excused herself and he wandered off to talk to one of the other girls.

She noticed the minister was not present. Didn't he want a wife and mother for Matthew? Perhaps he meant it when he said none of the women would be interested in a man with a child. If the kind-hearted minister thought that, did that mean men thought the same way about a woman with a child? What chance for her then?

She forced a smile and talked with every man there as pleasantly as she could, even those she didn't think she would want, like Mr. Traveland. He was very gruff and she doubted he would tolerate a baby that wasn't his.

By the evening's end, she was exhausted and her smile had frozen on her face. Back in her room, she removed the green skirt and blouse and readied for bed.

Cassandra stormed in. "That was upsetting."

"So true, but why did you find it so? From where I stood you appeared to have found several prospective beaus." Angeline pulled on her nightgown.

"Sure, one was wealthy and one melted me with his smile. Unfortunately, not the same man." Cassandra undressed for bed.

Climbing between the covers, Angeline asked, "Are you determined to marry money? Why can't you settle for melting you with his smile?"

Cassandra lowered the lamp's wick and pulled up the cover. "No, thank you. Lydia said there are wealthy men in this little town and I intend to marry one of them."

"I haven't that luxury." She rolled to her side and burrowed into her pillow.

***

Grady shut the door on Mrs. Callahan who had come to extol the merits of a wife and suggest he meet the Bride Brigade girls. Spare him from the meddling of another matchmaker. This was the third well-meaning matron since Lydia had returned with the Bride Brigade in tow. He sat in his study trying to compose his sermon when a knock on the door sent him striding irritably to answer the summons.

"Oh, Miss Chandler. Won't you come in?" He smiled and gestured toward the parlor.

She craned her neck toward the area where he'd set his son on her last visit. "Matthew here?"

"Mrs. Gallagher took him to her house today. Take a seat."

Miss Chandler sat on the sofa but appeared uncomfortable. "You said I could come and talk to you again if I needed to do so."

He gave what he hoped was an encouraging smile. "I meant that."

She sighed, obviously relieved. "I wondered if you counsel people who are torn by indecision?"

He sat down across from her. "Many times and I always do my very best to help. Tell me what's bothering you."

She toyed with a handkerchief she'd pulled from her sleeve. "Well, what if a person has had something very bad happen to her and there are consequences she can't change, things that society doesn't approve? I mean, if someone proposes to me, and I'm honest with him, will marrying him be all right?"

He had no idea what she was trying not to say. "Miss Chandler, I can't counsel you on vague terms. However, short of murdering someone, there are no consequences that can't be overcome. And even if you killed someone and genuinely ask God's forgiveness, then He forgives you." He raised his eyebrows. "You'd still have to deal with the laws of man, though."

She looked contrite. "I-I haven't killed anyone. Well, I almost killed myself, but I couldn't go through with it. Then Lydia found me and kept me from trying again."

His stomach hit his boots. This beautiful woman was so overcome by sorrow and guilt she had tried to kill herself? What terrible burden did she carry?

He reached across and took her hand. "There's nothing in this world worth killing yourself for. Nothing, do you understand? There's always a solution to every problem. Sometimes deciphering the way to proceed is difficult. Whatever you feel you've done wrong can be resolved."

She clasped his hand in both hers as if he'd thrown her a lifeline. "You don't think I'm doomed to unhappiness because of a mistake that happened before I came here?"

"Did you ask God's forgiveness?"

She nodded. "Every night and several times a day."

He withdrew his hand from hers and leaned back. "You've come here to start a new life. Be optimistic about your future. Start with forgiving yourself."

She appeared startled at the thought. "Forgive myself? Oh, I'd no idea I should. I was stupid to give my trust to the wrong person. I'm not sure I can forgive my part in the… event, but I promise to try."

After she'd gone, he wondered what she had to forgive of herself. She looked to be about twenty or maybe a couple of years older. She didn't have the drawl the other women had so she wasn't from Virginia.

With a shake of his head, he went back to writing his sermon.

He knew when Lydia did her shopping and errands and he decided he'd make a point of meeting her.

As he'd planned on the next day, Grady was waiting for Lydia as she exited the mercantile. He bowed and gestured to the bench.

With a smile she took a seat. "Is this your new office, Grady? I must admit you have a lovely view."

He sat beside her and gazed beyond the dusty street to the blue-green hills rising above the town. Above them a deep blue sky promised a bright day with no rain.

"I'm concerned about one of your Bride Brigade. I know you keep your counsel, Lydia, but what's wrong with Miss Chandler?"

Lydia pressed her lips in a line for a few seconds then met his gaze. "You know how I hate gossip but, well, you are our minister and you're not judgmental. I suppose I can tell you. The problem is Angeline needs a husband. And she needs one soon."

He felt like an idiot. Why hadn't he figured that out? "I see. That's a shame. She seems like a nice girl."

"She's delightful. But, you know one blemish is all that's needed to ruin a young woman's life even if she'd not to blame. She's promised to explain her predicament before she accepts a man. The problem is, she's so skittish that I doubt she'll receive a marriage proposal until all the other girls have been spoken for. That may be too late for our purposes. I've assured her she's not obligated to accept any proposal because she can remain with me as long as necessary."

"Thank you for sharing with me." He wished he could help Miss Chandler. Who could he suggest for her? "She probably feels frightened and unlovable."

"That she does. And she's in a panic." Lydia rose and, with a pat to his shoulder, walked toward her home.

In turn, he strolled toward the McAdams house to check on Fiona McAdams. When he arrived, Miss Chandler was just leaving.

She looked fresh as the dew on a rose. "Good day, Reverend McIntyre. Mrs. McAdams is feeling a little better today." She leaned near and whispered, "So am I."

He watched the young woman walk away before he entered the McAdams home. "Miss Chandler tells me you're improving."

"Isn't she the sweetest girl? Imagine someone her age taking the time to call on me." Fiona laughed, something he hadn't seen her do in a long time, and slapped her leg. "Lands sakes, I forgot you're her age, but you're my minister."

"Has Doctor Gaston been by yet?"

"Not yet, but I don't think he needs to bother with me today. I'm feeling better. Miss Chandler—she said I should call her Angeline—made me take my medicine. I hate that stuff, but she said it's important for me to follow doctor's orders."

"She's right about that. Have you skipped your medicine often?"

A sly look crossed her face. "I might have in the past. But Angeline made me promise I'll take it faithfully now. She is such a sweet young woman."

"I'm grateful she extracted a promise from you. I'll hold you to it. I want to see you up dancing at the next party."

She clapped her hands together. "Oh, I'll bet Lydia will have a fancy dance soon. I sure don't want to miss it."

He left and continued his rounds. Visiting the elderly and ill was something he enjoyed. Not that he was glad people were ill, but he felt a visit cheered them. In addition to the ill, people often forgot about elderly who couldn't get around well.

When he returned home, Mrs. Gallagher met him at the door. "Your son is getting to be too much for me. You know I love the boy and think a lot of you, but you need to find someone younger to look after him. While we can use what you pay me, I can't tolerate this back ache or my shattered nerves."

Grady wanted to bang his head against the wall. He didn't need this news. "He get away from you again?"

"Yes, and headed for the road. I couldn't bear if me being slow caused him to come to harm. You just need to find another sitter for him, someone younger than me. I'll give you a few days, but that's all."

Mrs. Gallagher left and Grady clasped his son to him. How he loved the boy. Matthew was a happy child, but so active he tired his father. No wonder Mrs. Gallagher was worn out.

He'd ask around but there was no one else. That's why he'd begged Mrs. Gallagher to stay on the job. She'd begun out of pity when his wife had died and continued for lack of a suitable replacement.

Matthew had been easier to corral then. Grady had thought then the main problem was diapers. Mrs. Gallagher had raised four children and wasn't put off by changing diapers or washing them.

He'd known she wasn't up to the task of chasing after a toddler. The woman was in her sixties, didn't walk well, and he figured she was a great-grandmother by now. He sank onto the rocker and held his son.

Why had his wife had to die? As a minister, he should have been able to handle that question. He still wrestled with why a lovely woman like his Georgia had been stricken with the painful and lingering effects of giving birth that stole her life.

He rocked his son and cried silently against Matthew's soft hair.

Chapter Five

Angeline enjoyed meeting all the people in town. Many of the women were older and had no children left nearby to visit them. She liked hearing their stories about pioneering in the area.

She was amazed at how brave some of them were. With some of her precious coins, she bought a tablet and pencil and started recording the stories they told her. She thought they would make a remarkable book of local history.

When they learned what she was doing, the people she visited were eager to tell her more stories. Each evening, she recorded what she'd heard that day. She described the memorabilia they showed her, things like clothes, sidesaddles, utensils, furniture and china carried across the country by wagon. The little sketches of the items were to help her memory.

She learned there was to be a performance at the Golden Crescent Opera House. How she wanted to attend. Lydia promised any girl not escorted could sit with her, the sheriff, and Sophie Gaston in Lydia's box. How humiliating that would be, but she was reconciled to be there.

The day before the performance, Elias Kendrick called at Lydia's. His dark red hair was perfectly groomed and his warm brown eyes echoed the smile he offered.

With her fingers crossed, she greeted him. "Lydia said you wished to speak to me, Mr. Kendrick."

"Would you do me the honor of dining with me tomorrow and then accompanying me to Miss Geraldine Chitwood's performance at the opera house?"

"I'd be delighted. I've never heard her perform."

"Then I'll call for you at six." He gave a mock bow.

"I'll look forward to the evening." But she was perplexed because she would have sworn he was interested in another woman.

Whatever the reason, she had an escort for the performance.

In their room later, Cassandra grilled her as they readied for bed. "I saw Mr. Kendrick speaking to you. He's quite a catch."

"You know he's not interested in me, but I'm grateful I won't be the only one of us sitting with Lydia and the sheriff tomorrow night."

"Wouldn't that be embarrassing?"

The next night, Angeline dressed in her remade velveteen suit and wore her pearls.

Cassandra dressed in her best too. "I can't believe how well our little sewing project turned out. You look like you stepped from the pages of *Godey's Ladies Magazine*. Those pearls are the perfect touch."

"I was afraid I'd have to sell them and I still may. For now, though, they're mine and they do look good with this suit, don't they?"

"I've helped several of the girls with their hair, now I barely have time to get ready."

"When I first met you, I thought you were snobbish and stuck up, and I apologize for thinking that of you. You're really very generous with your talents."

"I just have a knack for a few things. You do too."

Surprised, she stared at her roommate. "Me, what?"

"A lot of people are talking about how nice you are. I heard several people at church whispering your virtues."

Angeline rolled her eyes. "That will soon change, won't it?"

Cassandra tightened an ear screw. "You're nice, Angeline. No matter what else happens, that's a fact."

Angeline sensed tears welling. "Thank you, but don't be so kind or you'll make me cry. You know how weepy I get."

Cassandra rolled her eyes. "Don't I ever? Go on downstairs and wait for your gentleman."

Elias Kendrick arrived soon after she entered the parlor. Everything about him spoke of money. He offered his arm. "Shall we go?"

They strolled toward the café. He was just under six feet and a sharp dresser. Other couples ahead and behind them were heading toward the same destination.

Searching for conversation, she said, "The café will be crowded this evening."

"They bring in extra tables and chairs, but there'll be a line waiting to be seated. I hope we get there early enough for a table without delay."

"I'm sure you're eager to get to the opera house. Do you have to go backstage or do any of the chores associated with a performance?"

He grinned broadly. "Nothing. I'm fortunate enough to have hired Jim Baxter and he manages everything."

At the café, they were shown to a tiny table in a corner. Nearby, Josephine sat with the man who owned the mercantile. She and Josephine exchanged smiles.

Mr. Kendrick said, "There's only one choice on nights like this so that speeds service. Martha is the woman who seated us and she's half of the couple who owns the café. Her husband Lonnie is the main cook.

"Is this the only place in town to dine?"

He tugged at his ear. "Well, we serve a few dishes at the saloon, but this is the only place for ladies."

She couldn't think of what to say after that. Certainly, she was in no position to look down on someone who owned a saloon. Fortunately, their food arrived.

She picked up her fork. "My, this smells delicious."

He cut into his meat. "They do pretty well, but then so does Mrs. Murphy."

"Oh, yes, she is a wonder. She intimidates me, but she definitely is a good cook."

A line had formed at the door.

She needed to get conversation flowing. Years of helping with her parent social events had prepared her. Get the other person talking about himself. "How did you decide to build the opera house?"

His face came alive with interest. "People complained there was no entertainment in Tarnation except for the occasional event hosted by Lydia. Even then, not many people could attend. I thought an opera house with a wide variety of acts would be a good addition to our community."

"You're right. I love the theater. I plan to make Tarnation my home so whether there was an opera house or not wouldn't affect my decision to stay. I'm so glad you've built one, though."

"Glad to know you're here to stay. We're fortunate Lydia had the idea to recruit young women for Tarnation. We need young families."

Angeline chuckled. "Actually, I think Sophie Gaston is responsible. She was afraid her son would move to Fort Worth and she wanted to keep him here."

"Well, it may work. I saw him leave just now with one of the young ladies of the Bride Brigade."

"Isn't that a ridiculous name? Makes us sound like a military campaign."

He raised his eyebrows. "When Lydia Harrison makes up her mind to do something, it takes on the similarities of one. She is very organized and not easily dissuaded."

She offered a genuine smile. "I hope you don't believe you're telling me something I haven't learned firsthand."

He laid his cutlery across his plate. "I guess you have at that. Are you ready to leave?"

"Yes, we shouldn't tie up the table since we've finished our meal."

They left the café and strolled the short distance to the Golden Crescent Opera House. The walk was interrupted a dozen times by people wanting to speak to her escort. He appeared very well-liked.

Marquee lanterns illuminated the entrance. Bright gold chrysanthemums decorated a red background at each side of the Chinese-styled entrance. In the lobby an easel held a large likeness of Geraldine Chitwood.

"Oh, she's beautiful."

"Wait until you see her in person. We were lucky to get her. Jim spoke to her at the perfect time. He's already signed her for next year, too."

As they went further inside, she gazed around. "What a surprise. The interior is so much larger than I guessed and quite tastefully decorated to give the right touch of opulence without overdoing it."

Her comment obviously pleased him. "I'm glad you approve. I'm proud of this place. I don't apologize for owning a saloon even though some may look down on me for that. The saloon allows me the money to do other things, things I never could have managed otherwise."

"You've done a wonderful service here, Mr. Kendrick. I

noticed that you priced the tickets so that everyone can afford to attend. That's kind of you, for everyone would strive to come."

"I want every person who wishes to be here able to buy a ticket. My box is up this way." He guided her up a curved staircase and to a box at the front of the theater.

She allowed him to seat her. "How lovely. This is the perfect spot to see a performance."

"I priced the boxes at a premium, but they're all sold for the season. The front seats on the first floor are a little pricier too, but those at the back are quite low as you mentioned. With the acoustics as they are, even those in the back row can hear."

"This is perfect. Although I wish I'd chosen a different ensemble. I clash with all the gorgeous reds."

"You look lovely, Miss Chandler. I'm sure I'm the envy of other men tonight."

"Oh, there's Lydia and the sheriff and Mrs. Gaston. I'm trying to conceal the fact I'm gawking but it's lovely to see several people I know in the audience."

"People watching is fun, isn't it? A hobby I enjoy myself." He gestured to men lowering the lights. "The man under Lydia's box is Jim Baxter, the manager. He gives free admission to the men who help him."

She couldn't help looking for the minister. But if everyone in town was at the performance then who would look after Matthew? She hoped someone so that Reverend McIntyre could attend.

The curtain opened and a man stepped on stage and sat at a grand piano.

Mr. Kendrick whispered, "That's Mr. Laurence, Miss Chitwood's accompanist."

As soon as the pianist was seated, Geraldine Chitwood came on stage in a stunning green gown studded with crystals. A diamond necklace graced her throat and Angeline thought there were diamonds in her elegantly styled red hair. The crowd applauded wildly.

The pianist played and the crowd quieted. When Miss Chitwood sang, not a person moved or spoke. Throughout her lengthy performance, Miss Chitwood stopped only twice to sip from a glass of water.

Angeline was mesmerized. She'd heard performers in great halls over the eastern half of the nation and in London. Never had she enjoyed any concert more than this one in a tiny Texas town.

When the entertainment was over, Angeline stood. "Thank you so much for inviting me, Mr. Kendrick. This was positively magical."

They were besieged by people telling them how wonderful the evening had been and asking about future attractions. Once they were on the street and walking toward Lydia's, Angeline took a deep breath and opened her fan.

"One thing I can't figure out is a way to cool the place properly. With dirt roads to combat, we can't book anyone for the months of bad weather when it would be more pleasant inside the theater."

"I was so enchanted I didn't notice I was overheated until Miss Chitwood left the stage. I could have used my fan if I hadn't been so enraptured with her voice."

"Did you expect to find something like this in Tarnation?"

"Never. Are all your performances this spectacular?"

He laughed. "Don't I wish they were? We have a variety. In two weeks, we'll have a group of acrobats. Two weeks after that, a Shakespeare company will appear and some of our residents will join as actors for small parts."

"That is varied. I suppose by the end of the season every person has seen his or her favorite type of show."

He nodded. "Precisely my intention. I usually enjoy them all."

"I'm sure most people will. Just because one isn't a favorite doesn't mean you don't enjoy seeing it."

"This is only our second season so Jim and I are still learning. Maybe by next year we'll have figured out a way to cool the place."

"I'm sure you will."

They'd arrived at Lydia's. Although he was an excellent escort, she didn't feel he was at all attracted to her any more than she was to him. Still, if he'd asked her, she would have accepted if he still wanted her after learning of her predicament.

"Well, here we are back at Lydia's." He escorted her to the door. "Thank you for coming with me tonight."

"Thank you for a lovely evening." What did he expect from her?

He leaned forward and kissed her on the cheek. "Goodnight, Miss Chandler."

"Goodnight, Mr. Kendrick." She opened the door before he

turned away.

In spite of the fact there was no special attraction, she glided to her room feeling much happier than she had in several months. Now she harbored hope for her future and that of her child. Why spending the evening with a man to whom she wasn't attracted could imbue her with this sensation, she had no idea. Perhaps she'd finally forgiven herself just as Reverend McIntyre had instructed.

Monday morning after Josephine had left for her job at the mercantile, Lydia announced that the following Friday evening would be a ball to which everyone in town was invited. "Not everyone will attend, of course, but there will be a crowd. We have a lot to do this week. This evening we'll have dancing lessons and practice."

"What about days?"

"I'm enlisting some of you to help with decorations. Also, the ballroom and the room we use for ladies to refresh themselves must receive extra cleaning. Mrs. Murphy and Mrs. Greenberg will let you know where help is needed."

She looked at her. "Angeline, you may feel free to carry on with visiting the sick and elderly. Of course, Josephine will be working at the mercantile each day. Mr. Ramirez will be sprucing up the gardens and could use the help of anyone who prefers working outdoors. The rest of us will be making decorations, polishing silver, and giving the place a close inspection."

Lorraine raised her hand. "I love gardening. Perhaps I could help Mr. Ramirez."

Lydia nodded. "Good but with your fair coloring, be sure to protect your skin. If you don't have work gloves and a sunbonnet, I can loan you mine."

Angeline hurried to complete her visits so she could help this afternoon. She also wanted to complete her gray foulard dress for the party. With only twenty-five cents to her name, she deliberated whether she might use a portion on trim for the dress.

At the home of Mrs. Eppes, she made tea for the kindly woman.

"What's new at Bridge Brigade headquarters?"

She set the teacup beside the kind lady. "There's a ball on Friday evening. Will you come?"

"Pshaw, not for me, but thanks for the invitation. What are you wearing?"

Angeline picked up her own cup. "I'm sewing a gray foulard dress from fabric I bought at the mercantile."

"I used to love sewing. Tell me the design."

Angeline set down her cup and explained with gestures.

Mrs. Eppes regarded her quizzically. "How are you trimming it?"

"Well, I don't really have any trim except a little black velvet I can either use as a collar or binding around the cuffs."

Mrs. Eppes pointed toward the back of the house. "Go into my bedroom and bring me the big box that has large roses on it and carry it to the kitchen."

Angeline did as requested and set the box on the table beside Mrs. Eppes' chair.

Her hostess rummaged in the carton. "Let's go through this. I can't sew now. Arthritis is a problem, plus I don't see as well as I used to. My stitches have to be too large. Ah, here's what I wanted."

The older woman pulled out a bundle of ribbon and lace. "These are odds and ends. Hmph, this lace needs a good bluing to bring back the white. Well, you take this box with you."

Angeline was astounded. "All of it? That's so much, Mrs. Eppes."

"Like I said, I can't sew anymore. Hate to see it go to waste."

Her new friend's generosity buoyed her spirits. "Oh, thank you so much. You're such a dear friend, Mrs. Eppes. I can't thank you enough for your kindness in letting me visit and now giving me this."

"Bless you, child. You've brightened my days since you've come to our town. I know the man who marries you will be getting a wonderful wife."

Angeline's eyes welled with tears. She leaned over and kissed Mrs. Eppes' cheek. "Meeting you was my lucky day." Then she tidied up the kitchen from their tea. "Is there anything else I can do for you while I'm here?"

"No, Mrs. Querado comes tomorrow."

"Then I'd better go and do my share at Lydia's so I can sew on my dress later. Maybe I'll have it finished for the ball and then wear it for church Sunday."

On the walk back to Lydia's, Angeline couldn't believe her luck. She was glad she hadn't stopped by the store on the way to Mrs. Eppes'. Now she still had her coins for an emergency. A very small one.

Back in her room, she deposited the box on the bed and started sorting.

Cassandra came in. "Did I see you carrying a large box?"

"Mrs. Eppes, bless her heart, gave me all these trims. Even buttons. There's enough for both of us if you want to make something for yourself. Oh, your clothes are so elegant and plentiful, you don't need anything else, do you?"

Cassandra rolled her eyes. "Women always need more clothes, Angeline. I don't intend to sew mine, though I'll be happy to help you."

"Oh, well, someone might want to share them. At any rate, I have all I need to trim the gray dress."

Angeline knew how to do the dances Lydia wanted all the girls to learn, so she helped each evening. Sophie Gaston played piano and Lydia and the girls danced their hearts out.

Thursday evening as they prepared for bed, Cassandra said, "We've really set this house ringing to the rafters with laughter and silliness."

"I've had such fun this week. And my dress is finished. All I have to do is press it tomorrow and it's ready to wear."

"You did a really nice job on the trim. White lace and black ribbon makes it dressier. Lucky for you to be given that box."

"Extremely. Thank you for your help. I didn't know about tapes to tie and allow for expansion. You know so much about everything."

Cassandra slipped on her nightgown. "No, I know a little about a lot of things. Glad I could help. Now, I'm dead on my dancing feet. Goodnight."

Angeline crawled into bed and sighed. She'd have a new dress for the ball. She only hoped she'd have at least one or two partners.

On Friday, she didn't visit any of her friends around town. Lydia kept her busy with preparations for the ball. Though she didn't mention the fact to anyone, she thought calling it a ball was a bit far-fetched. Tonight would be a nice party in a ballroom, but not what she thought of as a ball. Nevertheless, girls dashed to their rooms to get ready.

Chapter Six

Angeline admired Cassandra's blue dress she hadn't worn while Angeline had known her.

"Your dress makes your eyes look even brighter. That's a great choice for the ball."

After checking her hair one last time, Cassandra turned. "Yours looks even nicer since you've pressed it. My word, you look as if an exclusive dressmaker stitched that for you."

"Let's face it, we look breathtaking." Angeline felt lovely, even though her stomach was developing a definite bump.

Cassandra tilted her head as if in thought. "I hear men's footsteps in the hall. Shall we go or make an entrance?"

"I believe we'd better go act as hostesses as instructed. After all Lydia's done for us I sure don't want to disappoint her."

They joined those filing into the ballroom. Musicians on the small stage tuned their instruments, except the pianist.

Cassandra said, "Oh, we have musicians instead of Sophie. I wonder who they are?"

"The man with the banjo is Fabian Dubicki who owns the livery stable. Colin Gallagher playing the violin is really a carpenter. His wife takes care of the minister's little boy part time. Brendan Callahan who owns the furniture store is at the piano. The man with the guitar is Vance Wood who works as a cowboy for Martin Traveland."

Cassandra stared at her. "My stars, you sound as if you've lived here all your life."

"I barely met Mr. Wood when I saw him at the mercantile while visiting Josephine. I don't know Mr. Callahan but I recognize him from his wife's description. I've met the others during the time we've been here on my walks around town."

"And visiting people right and left. I have to say you're fitting in better than any of us except Josephine. She's met a lot of people too."

Angeline squeezed her friend's arm. "You should come with me to visit sometime. You might love it as much as I do."

"Uh uh, I'll just keep waiting for Prince Charming to sweep me off my feet and into a life of luxury."

She nudged Cassandra's arm. "Oh, here he comes now."

Cassandra sighed. "No, that's Prince Too Charming But Broke."

The rancher approached them and bowed. "Good evening, ladies. You're both looking lovely."

Angeline smiled at the cowboy. "Hello, Mr. Drummond. How are you this evening?"

He nodded at her then held out his hand to Cassandra. "May I have this dance, Miss Bradford?"

She placed her hand in his. "Delighted."

Angeline watched them glide onto the floor. She grew panicky. What if no one asked her to dance? What if they suspected she was with child and shied away from her?

"You're looking lovely tonight, Miss Chandler."

A gasp of delight escaped. "Reverend McIntyre, you're here. How nice to see you."

He held out his hand. "May I have this dance?"

She reached for him as if he extended a lifeline and she was drowning. "I'd like that. I was afraid no one would ask me."

He chuckled. "You needn't worry about that. I was racing a couple of men to get to you first."

She gazed at him skeptically. "Nice of you to say, but you'll get a blister on your tongue for lying. Then, how will you speak on Sunday?"

He held his tongue stiff and said, "I'll thalk lak thiss."

She laughed as he twirled her across the room.

When the waltz began, he shook his head. "I don't know this one."

She kept hold of his hand. "I can show you."

"You know how to waltz?"

She smiled at his shocked expression. "Don't look so scandalized. Lydia gave us dance lessons this week. Some of the men took them too. I think either Mrs. Lyons or Mrs. Hill gave them."

"Yes, but I couldn't get there."

"Look, it's easy. You just make a little box with your feet. See, one together, two together, three together, four. Then you can turn or do fancy stuff, but you just keep making the box as you go around the room. Remember, if you bump into someone you're their minister and they have to forgive you."

He grinned. "I guess I can try. Can we go over there to the side so I don't trip anyone but you?"

She followed him to a corner of the room. "You won't. You learned the other dances so you can learn this one."

She let him lead but he was so busy looking at his feet he lost count. "Just look at me and I'll count for you. Okay?"

"How can you expect me to concentrate on my feet while looking at a beautiful woman?"

She gazed into his lovely hazel eyes. "What a nice thing to say but you don't get off that easily. I expect you to concentrate as we go...one together, two together, three together, four."

Soon he'd caught on and braved a bit further onto the floor. "This is nicer than I'd thought. I see from watching some of the couples that the waltz can be quite fancy."

"We had a lot of fun learning. Of course, there was a lot of room and we could be as grandiose as we wished."

He grinned as he twirled her. "I can imagine eight young women giggling and twirling."

"Oh, you can't imagine how much laughter and silliness. Lydia is so kind and her home is elegant yet comfortable. I'm lucky she found me."

His eyebrows raised. "I thought you girls found her."

She's hinted to him but couldn't come right out and tell him how Lydia had saved her. "Well, I guess we found each other. However you put it, I'm fortunate to be here."

The dance ended and he guided her to the refreshment table. "Could we get some punch and sit out the next dance so I can talk to you?"

Her pulse surged. Was he going to propose?

They gathered cups and small plates of finger foods and found a place to sit.

She wondered aloud, "Who's watching Matthew?"

"Mrs. Ramirez. She fills in at the café when needed, but she wasn't needed with so many people coming here."

"I saw Mrs. McAdams made it. She wanted to come in the worst way."

He took a sip of punch. "So she said. She also told me you made her promise to take her medicine. Riley Gaston has been trying to get her to follow his instructions for months."

She flashed him a smile. "Doctor Gaston didn't know he was dealing with a party girl at heart."

"There's something I want to ask you."

Oh, she wanted so badly for him to propose. "Whatever you have in mind, tell me."

"Would you consent to be Matthew's nanny while I'm out of the house? Mrs. Gallagher simply isn't able to any longer."

Her hopes plummeted. She held back tears and stared at the plate in her lap.

He leaned down to peer into her face. "Have I insulted you? I meant no disrespect. I know how kind you are and could think of no one I'd rather have caring for my son."

She forced a smile. "I-I'm honored you trust me, Reverend McIntyre. You know I think Matthew is adorable. Tell me what hours you have in mind."

"I thought about four hours a day. You let me know when. I haven't visited outside town as often as I'd like recently. I can pay you, of course, though not as much as your time is worth. My salary isn't large, but I feel called to serve this community."

At least she would be helping someone who needed her aide. "The pay isn't important. And I'd still have time to do my own visiting and help Lydia."

"Then you'll care for him?" He leaned back with a wide smile. "What a relief off my mind. Mrs. Gallagher said she won't be able to watch him any longer. She wants to go visit her daughter in Cleburne."

So she was really helping Mrs. Gallagher as well as the minister. "I'll come Monday unless you need me tomorrow."

"I stay at home on Saturdays unless there's a special request like a wedding or funeral or sudden illness."

"All right, then we're all set. I'll come at eight on Monday." She gave what she hoped was a cheerful-looking smile. She'd learned long ago from her parents how to sparkle on demand.

"Thank you, Miss Chandler. You have no idea how much I

appreciate your agreeing to help me. And I also recognize how much you've already contributed to Tarnation's residents."

The banker approached. "Say, preacher, you can't monopolize this pretty girl all evening. May I have this dance, Miss Chandler?"

Angeline stood. "Excuse me, Reverend McIntyre." She took Mr. Tucker's arm and they joined other dancers.

Grady watched her glide away with Bart Tucker. He knew he'd upset her, but he hadn't meant asking her to nanny as an insult. She'd already said she liked kids and she'd appeared to enjoy Matthew when she met him.

He stood and walked to where Lydia and Adam sat with their punch.

Lydia looked at him and frowned. "You look upset. Everything all right?"

"Not upset, just puzzled. Miss Chandler appeared to be enjoying our conversation but when I asked her to be nanny for Matthew, she seemed to withdraw. I didn't mean to upset her."

Lydia looked annoyed with him.

Before he could ask why, Adam said, "Aw, Grady, she probably figured you were going to ask her to marry you. Good thing you didn't. I think she ought to marry Elias. They'd make a good pair."

He blurted, "Are you crazy?" He wished he could recall his words but the thought of Miss Chandler with Elias Kendrick upset him. "I heard they went to Miss Chitwood's performance together, but Elias is wrong for her."

In spite of the odd smile Lydia offered, she appeared annoyed with him. "And who do you think is right for Miss Chandler?"

"I...I don't know, but not Elias. I'll think about the subject and get back to you." He took out his pocket watch. "Oh, I told Mrs. Ramirez I wouldn't be late so I'd better be on my way. I enjoyed the ball."

He collected his hat and went home. He'd accomplished what he'd come for, so why wasn't he happier?

***

The next morning, Angeline approached Lydia. "Could I speak to you alone, please?"

Lydia touched her arm. "Let's go to my husband's office."

Angeline followed her hostess into the manly room. "Don't

you think you should call it your office by now?"

Lydia sighed and shook her head. "I've tried but I can't come into this room without picturing William sitting at the desk. He was a dynamic man and not easy to forget."

"Making the room yours wouldn't mean you forgot him. Do you believe he'd want this left as sort of a shrine?" Angeline gestured around the office.

Lydia stood in the center of the room and slowly turned in a circle. "Good Heavens, that's how the office appears, isn't it? That's not at all my intention."

She sat behind the desk and waved a hand to dismiss the comment. "That's a subject for another day. I can see you're upset. Tell me what's bothering you."

"Reverend McIntyre asked me to take care of his son when he's out calling on members of the congregation."

"And that upset you?"

"In a way. I'm honored he trusts me with his son's welfare." She heaved a sigh. "You see, when he said he had something he wanted to ask me, I thought he intended to propose."

"And instead he asked you to work for him. There's quite a difference in your mind and in mine, but he meant the request as a compliment."

She fiddled with the folds of her skirt, unable to meet her hostess' eyes. "Are you certain? I thought perhaps he viewed me as servile and unwholesome."

"Before Grady left last night, he spoke to Adam and me. He said he'd upset you but he didn't understand when or how. When he said he'd asked you to work for him, of course I knew why. Sometimes men are a bit dense, dear."

She raised her head enough to peek at Lydia. "You don't think he looks down on me?"

"He wouldn't ask you to care for Matthew if he did. He's only let two people ever care for his son, Doreen Gallagher and Lola Ramirez. If they aren't available, he takes Matthew with him or stays home. As a favor to me, I hope you won't back out, Angeline. Grady and Matthew need you and so does Doreen Gallagher."

That relieved her mind. "Oh, then that's all right. I told Reverend McIntyre I'd be at his home at eight o'clock Monday morning. He said he'd still give me time to visit my friends around town."

"I know they count on you cheering them up. You're doing a lot of good for our town. I'm very glad you're here."

"Thank you, Lydia. I come from a home where a daughter is thought of as a commodity to impress business associates. Hearing you say you're glad I'm here is balm for many wounds."

Chapter Seven

Monday morning at eight o'clock, Angeline knocked on the parsonage door. She wore her green skirt and blouse.

The minister answered without his waistcoat or jacket. His collar was undone and he wasn't wearing a tie.

Taking in his disheveled state, she asked, "Am I too early?"

He stepped back to admit her, a wide smile on his face. "Right on time. Thank you for agreeing to help with Matthew. I'm running behind, as you can see. I put Matthew in his crib."

"Where is that?"

He indicated another room with a nod. "Follow me. I'm afraid he's in a fussy mood, which is why I'm not ready for the day yet."

"Have you both had breakfast?"

He glanced over his shoulder. "We had oatmeal an hour ago."

They entered the little boy's room. He stood in his bed jabbering. When he saw his father he raised his arms and said, "Daddy, want down."

Angeline lifted him. "How about Angeline? Will I do, Matthew?"

This morning she'd plaited her hair and let the braid hang free. Matthew seized the pigtail like a rock climber with a rope. He laughed and tugged then put the hair in his mouth as he jabbered more.

"Why don't you show Angeline where your clothes and toys are kept?" She looked at the minister. "Does he take two naps or one?"

"He has one nap at about half past noon. Mrs. Gallagher left detailed instructions which you can follow or not. I only promised to give them to you." He handed her a list from the bureau by the crib.

She accepted the long list, grateful to have the help offered. "By now she's no doubt devoted to him."

"Seems to be but her hips and back bother her and make caring for him difficult. I plan to be back by noon unless something unexpected occurs. Sorry, I've no way to send word if I'm going to be late."

She tickled Matthew and sent Reverend McIntyre a mischievous grin. "If you're not back by dark, I'll call the sheriff."

"Thanks, Miss Chandler. I'll finish dressing and be on my way. Matthew's fine without me unless he sees me go out the door, so I won't come back in to tell you I'm leaving."

"Have a pleasant day, Reverend McIntyre. Your lovely son and I will be fine."

Grady hastily dressed and left the parsonage. Having Miss Chandler in his home was much different from Mrs. Gallagher or Mrs. Ramirez. He couldn't explain away the sensations he'd just experienced but he knew he had to get his baser emotions under control.

Seeing Angeline, for that's how he'd come to think of her, holding a laughing Matthew created yearnings he thought he'd mastered after Georgia's death. He definitely didn't need more complications in his life. Angeline was supposed to solve a problem, not create a larger one.

He met Riley Gaston on what passed for a sidewalk. "Hello, Grady. Heard you've a new nanny for your boy."

Grady stared at his friend. "How on earth has that news traveled already? Miss Chandler only started working for me a few minutes ago."

Riley laughed. "Fiona McAdams passed me the news. Said Miss Chandler told her at church that she'd still call on her but at a different time. You've made a good choice there."

"Mrs. Gallagher simply had to resign. She wants to visit her daughter in Cleburne. Besides, I think chasing after Matthew was causing her to be ill."

"For a fact it was. Have to say if Miss Chandler sticks with her job, I'll be surprised. Those girls in the Bride Brigade came to find husbands not chase after a kid that's not theirs. You can bet about the time your boy gets used to her, someone will snap her up for his wife."

The notion he'd lose her stirred unpleasant emotions he fought to extinguish. "You may be right. In the meantime, she seems to have charmed a lot of our church members. I hope she works the same magic on Matthew."

The doctor nodded. "While she's here, she's made my job

easier by getting several of my patients to take their medicine and eat properly. Hope she marries someone in town and continues her visits."

They parted and Grady went on his way to the livery where he asked Fabian to ready the little buggy he used to visit congregation members who lived outside town. Soon he was on his way north of Tarnation. He couldn't get Riley's comment out of his mind.

He wasn't naïve enough to believe Miss Chandler would have difficulty finding a husband. The image disturbed him more than he wanted to admit. Stupid, he told himself, because he had no claim on her.

Should he speak for her? No, he had no right. He had a small salary from the church and his job here depended on the approval of a church board in Indiana. If Harlie Jackson had his way, there would soon be a new minister for Tarnation.

Although far from picturesque, Grady enjoyed living in Tarnation. Except for one or two malcontents, good people made up the town. The place was growing and soon there'd be other children.

Who knew if the Bride Brigade might write favorably and recruit friends to travel here in search of a husband or home or both? He admitted to himself he was an optimist. In his head he visualized the town with a school filled with children and the church filled to the walls.

Drat his luck. His picture included Angeline Chandler smiling up at him from a front pew. Right now he had to rein himself in or he'd make a fool of himself and drive away his son's nanny.

He visited four homes in the rural area. Had he brought a lunch, he could have talked to more. Perhaps next time, he'd do that. Now, he looked forward to returning home. He took out his watch and realized he'd miss seeing Matthew before his nap.

When he had returned the buggy and horse to the livery, he strode home. Although he'd told her he might be late, he hadn't intended to be. He didn't want Angeline thinking he was taking advantage of her good nature on her first day.

He opened the door to a wonderful smell. Inhaling deeply, he paused in the entry and his stomach rumbled.

"You're home, Reverend McIntyre. I have your dinner waiting for you in the kitchen. Matthew's already eaten and is having his nap."

"I didn't intend for you to cook for me. I admit I'm happy you did." He placed a hand at his middle. "Once I inhaled that aroma, my stomach is protesting for food."

"I'm not used to your range, but the chicken and dumplings didn't turn out badly, if I do say so myself. I've made better biscuits, but perhaps you'll be charitable."

He hung his jacket over a chair and sat at the table where she'd set a place. What a treat to come home and find a warm meal waiting for him.

"Have you eaten? If not, perhaps you'll join me."

"I had a few bites with Matthew." She laughed and stared at stains on the front of her clothes. "He does enjoy his food. But I'll sit with you so you have company for your meal."

She took a seat and he offered a quick blessing for the meal and the hands that prepared the food.

"How nice of you to include me in the blessing."

"Please accept my apology for Matthew's enthusiasm." He dug into the large serving of chicken and dumplings. While he chewed, he buttered a biscuit.

What should he say? Her top appeared new though he'd seen her wear it before. "I'll reimburse you for laundering your clothes. Mrs. Diaz does a nice job."

"Thank you, but I don't do too badly myself. Lydia has been training us in all the housekeeping skills we don't yet have."

"And what are you learning?" He was surprised to know she knew how to cook He'd pegged her as from a wealthy home. He took a bite of the chicken and savored the flavor.

"Oh, laundry was the main thing. I'm not good at ironing. Anything to do with an iron defeats me. Still, a wife has to press clothes so I'm trying."

Her speech offered a clue to her upbringing. Probably a tutor and then attended a fancy girls' school. "Your family had servants?"

"Yes, but I learned my way around the kitchen from our cook. Later I took a course in cooking more elaborate foods. I prefer the simple and filling type."

"Good, because that's about the only type ingredients you'll find in Tarnation. Lydia has the only fancy dinner parties I know of in our town. I suppose she has Michael send away for some of the items she serves." He took another bite of biscuit. "Oh, my, this tastes good."

"I'm pleased you're enjoying my effort. Another time after I'm more used to your kitchen, I'll fry a chicken. I'll bet Matthew would like a drumstick or the part of the wing that's similar."

"If I weren't so full of dumplings, my mouth would water. Fried chicken is my favorite meal, with mashed potatoes and gravy and warm bread. Ah, that's my idea of a perfect meal."

She leaned forward, her gray eyes sparkling. "And I'm sure you meant to include a vegetable or two in that list."

He grinned. "If I must, but not necessary."

"You're a parent now and have to set an example for your son. Children mimic everything. I've heard you say a sermon lived is more effective than a sermon preached."

He held up a hand and laughed. "Guilty. You turned my own words against me."

She giggled. "I certainly did, didn't I? What you need, Reverend McIntyre, is a wife."

He raised his eyebrows and leaned toward her. "Oh? I'm listening."

She put her hands on either side of her cheeks, which had turned bright red. "Good Heavens, you can't think I meant me. How embarrassing. Please forget I ever said that."

He chuckled. "At least I know you've been paying attention to my sermons. In fact, seeing you in church is reassuring. You appear to listen to my every word."

"Of course I do."

"My dear Miss Chandler, you have no idea how many people doze off, or jot notes, or stare out the window. At times I wish I were too nearsighted to realize I'm not holding the congregation in thrall."

"I can understand how disconcerting that would be. When my mother was a girl, she said the minister would call out the name of anyone he thought wasn't paying attention. I'd hate that."

"I wouldn't intentionally embarrass anyone at a service. On occasion, I've spoken to people in private."

"Did that help?"

He shrugged. "For a month or so. People are what they are."

"As pleasant as talking to you is, I had better get on my way so I can see Mrs. Eppes before I go to Lydia's. We're getting ready for the next social. I hope you'll come on Friday."

"I'll see how the week goes." But he knew he wouldn't be able to resist a chance to speak with her socially instead as her employer.

ANGELINE

***

In the room they shared that evening, Cassandra asked, "Well, Nanny Angeline, how did your day go?"

Angeline plopped back on the bed. "I put my foot in my mouth." She explained.

"Why couldn't you marry him? You were hoping he'd ask. For goodness sakes, you've extolled his virtues since you met him."

"He needs someone nice and…well, like Ophelia. She'd be a perfect minister's wife. I'm tainted, a fallen woman."

"Don't give me that nonsense. A minister should be the first one to overlook your little problem."

"My 'little' problem is growing. I'm afraid I'll be the only unwed of our Bride Brigade and will end up having to sell my pearls."

"Lydia won't turn you out."

"There'll be doctor expenses and clothes for a baby and a crib. I've added it up and the numbers of things I'll need are staggering."

"So, marry the preacher. He already has a crib and probably diapers and most of the other stuff his son is finished with. You said he needs a wife."

"I wish it were that simple. He's too nice to be saddled with my problems. Besides, there are already two men who want to get him ousted."

"You drive me crazy sometimes. Go to sleep. Maybe a fairy godmother will appear in the morning."

Angeline snuggled under the sheet. "She already has. Her name is Lydia Harrison."

***

On Friday evening, Angeline dressed in her gray foulard dress and took special care. Cassandra helped her.

Angeline turned her head to get the effect of her hair style. "You're so good to help me with my hair. Now, shall I work on yours?"

Her friend clasped her hands and sat in the chair Angeline had vacated. "That would be nice. I love having my hair done by someone else."

When they were both ready, they went downstairs together. Angeline spotted the preacher immediately. She thought of him as Grady, although she would never call him by his first name. He was talking to the sheriff.

51

Their discussion looked heated. She heard Adam say, "Then you'd damn well better speak up because I'll do all I can to send things in the opposite direction."

She glided up as Lydia tapped each of the two men on the arm. "Gentlemen, please remember ladies are present."

Angeline paused beside Lydia. "Am I interrupting something?"

Grady turned with a smile. "Not at all." He extended his arm. "Shall we get refreshments? I believe Mrs. Murphy outdid herself this evening. Did you help?"

She lowered her eyes. "I made the empanadas. I hope you like them. Mrs. Ramirez showed me how but this is the first time I've tried creating them."

He reached for one from a tray Josephine carried. He bit into the tiny pie. "Amazing. I could eat a plate of them."

"That's why Josephine is taking the tray around. There are enough for everyone to have two or three, but we were afraid a couple of men with hearty appetites would deplete them."

He picked up a plate and heaped it with finger sandwiches and cookies. "Adam tells me you've gone out with Elias Kendrick. Is that where your interest lies?"

She gave a shake of her head when Grady offered her the plate and prepared one of her own. "Although he was very pleasant and a perfect gentleman, I'm not interested in Mr. Kendrick nor he with me. I have no idea why he invited me to the opera house. If the sheriff is pushing him towards me then that would explain a lot."

He gestured with his punch cup. "Why don't we take our food and go sit on a bench outside?"

She led the way. "Sounds nice. The almanac predicts rain later in the week, but tonight is lovely."

"So you read the about the weather, do you?"

"Mrs. Eppes has me read to her. She can't see the small print any longer. Neither can Mrs. Arrenton. I'm reading her *Little Women*. Reading is so important, don't you agree? Not being able to enjoy a book would be awful."

"You have a lot of compassion for others."

She smiled at him. "You said we should. In fact, you mentioned that very thing last Sunday."

He shook his head. "I suspect yours has always been there. That quality is not one that suddenly appears because one day you heard a sermon."

She nudged him with her shoulder. "Don't sell yourself short. You're a very forceful preacher. You don't need to yell to get across your message."

"I'd like to think so, but I don't delude myself that I'm powerful or charismatic. I'll bet in…wherever you lived—"

"Missouri. I lived in Missouri."

"I'd wager that in Missouri, you were working with some charity or other."

"A couple, but I didn't visit those trapped at home. No one ever mentioned their need and I simply didn't consider them. I thought about orphaned children and homeless who were without food or a safe place to sleep."

He pretended to be dejected. "I thought so. Now I'm disillusioned that my sermons didn't convert you to serve mankind."

She giggled. "You are not."

He set his cup and plate at the end of the bench. "Miss Chandler. I'd like your permission to pay you court. I think we would do well together."

She scooted away. How she wished she could say yes, but she thought too much of this fine man to cause him more problems. "Me? Oh, no, you mustn't. You need a fine upstanding woman who will set an example and be a plus to your ministry."

"You just described yourself."

"No, Grad…Reverend McIntyre, you don't understand all my problems. I'd be a liability that Mr. Jackson and Mr. McGinnis would use as a weapon against you."

"Those two are not worth considering. They'll always find something about me to criticize."

"I-I haven't told you why I needed forgiveness. Please, believe me when I say I'd harm your standing in the community."

He took her hand. "I know about your… situation, Miss Chandler. I watched my wife as she carried our son. I recognize the symptoms."

She covered her face with her free hand. "I'm so humiliated and ashamed. Please, Reverend McIntyre, go before I turn so weepy you'll accuse me of watering the garden."

With a gentle squeeze of her hand, he stood. His voice came soft and filled with compassion, "I'll go for now, but I'll look forward to seeing you in church on Sunday."

She sat alone for several minutes fighting for calm. When she'd composed herself enough to face people, she picked up the two plates and cups and made her way to the kitchen. For the rest of the evening, she washed cups and plates and tidied for Mrs. Murphy. When everyone had gone and leftover food put away, she hung her apron on the hook and climbed the back stairs.

She managed to control her tears until she reached her room. Pushing by Cassandra, she sat in the chair and sobbed.

Cassandra put an arm around her shoulders and leaned down. "What on earth happened to cause this reaction? I saw you and the preacher go into the garden. Everything looked promising."

Between sobs, she said, "He asked to court me. I wanted to say yes but couldn't let him ruin his life."

"Now I know you're mad. Marrying him would be perfect. You and he like the same things, you love his son. I simply don't understand you."

"Grady McIntyre is the finest man I've ever known. I can't let him ruin his reputation and possibly his professional standing by marrying me. Look at me, I'm showing. I'm surprised the other girls haven't confronted me about my weight gain."

"So you're looking as if you're expecting. If the preacher doesn't care, why can't you say yes to him? Who better to accept you without criticizing you?"

"Please, Cassandra, don't say anything else. I feel just awful."

Cassandra threw her hands in the air. "All right, get ready for bed. Life is sure to look better tomorrow."

Chapter Eight

Yesterday, Angeline had sent Grady a tremulous smile in church but had avoided talking to him. Now that Monday had arrived, she hurried to his home to care for Matthew. She wondered what she would say to the minister she wanted to protect from blame.

He opened the door and bade her enter. "I'll be gone all day. I'm sorry to spring this on you, but a family in the corner of the county has requested a visit. They sent a note by Jo Jo when he delivered their ice. Old Mr. Hopkins is sick and probably dying. Riley's already gone out there. Are you willing to stay until late afternoon?"

"Of course. I wish I'd known so I could send them something. A gift of food when there's trouble is always a blessing. Perhaps you could stop by the café and ask if they have a cake or pie or perhaps a bit of stew for their dinner."

"I suspect the stew would be most welcome. The family hasn't much but they share what they have. Thanks for the idea."

He put on his hat and closed the door as he left. He was one of the few men in town who didn't wear a western-style hat. Instead, his was small-brimmed and grey.

What should she prepare for supper and for Matthew's lunch? She set the boy on the kitchen floor and gave him a wooden spoon and upturned pan. He laughed as he banged on his makeshift drum.

She took another spoon and banged with him. "Do you want Angeline to play too?"

"Angel play." He laughed and banged harder.

"You said my name. Yes, Angeline. Can you say the whole word? Angeline."

He shook his head. "Angel."

"Well, close enough, Matthew. Wait until I tell your daddy you can say my name. Won't he be surprised?"

"Daddy. Want Daddy."

"Oh, no, he'll come home soon. We have to cook for him. Will you help me?"

He reached up his arms. "Help Angel."

Carrying him, Angeline checked the larder and the ice box. Left over roast, probably from Sunday, would be good for Matthew's and her lunch. She wanted to fry chicken for Grady's supper. Her purse held money he'd paid her on Friday for her first week.

She peered at the little boy who'd captured her heart. "Would you like to go for a walk, Matthew? Let's get you to the potty and then we can go find some candy."

She washed his face and hands and tickled his tummy. "You're a good boy. We'll go get a chicken to cook for your supper."

He clapped his hands. "Chicken goes cluck cluck."

She held his hand and let him set the pace. He'd likely tire soon and she'd have to carry him, but the walk would be good for him. They drew stares as they went to the butcher shop but she merely smiled and nodded at those they passed.

No sooner had she reached the board walkway that connected several stores than she met Mrs. Jackson. Angeline's stomach knotted and she dreaded encountering the woman.

Lizzie Jackson stopped her. "What are you doing with the preacher's son?"

"Mrs. Gallagher can no longer care for him so I'm acting as nanny. We're on our way to buy a fryer for dinner."

Mrs. Jackson's expression was even more prunish than usual. "I don't approve of a young single woman in the home of our preacher."

"I'm only there a few hours on weekdays while Reverend McIntyre is away. I still live at Mrs. Harrison's."

"Harrumph. Foolish idea her bringing in a bunch of women to parade around like circus attractions."

"She's trying to help the town, Mrs. Jackson. Surely you don't want all the young men to move away. The town would die under those circumstances."

"There ought to be a more respectable way for them to marry."

"I assure you we are all respectable women. If you take the time to get to know the other six, you'll learn they are each very nice and have high morals."

"Be that as it may, I don't approve. Lydia Harrison has always been too flamboyant and this latest stunt of hers takes the cake."

"I'm sorry you feel that way. Mrs. Harrison is the finest woman I've ever met. Good day, Mrs. Jackson." She lifted Matthew to stride away from the vitriolic woman. Meeting her had put a pall on an otherwise beautiful day. She composed herself before setting the child back down and opening the butcher shop door.

Mr. Horowitz smiled at Matthew. "That's a nice escort you have there, Miss. You have him working up an appetite."

She glanced down at Matthew, wondering what the butcher thought of her bringing in her charge. "He is a fine boy, isn't he? I'll take the nicest frying chicken you have."

Mr. Horowitz wrapped the bird in paper and tied the package with string. "Sounds as if the preacher will be happy to have a good meal. Ja, he loves fried chicken, he does. From what he's told me, his attempts fall short."

"I didn't know he'd tried. I thought Matthew would enjoy a drumstick." She put the chicken in the basket she carried.

Mr. Horowitz's hearty laugh relaxed her. "That he will. Boys need food with a handle."

With a genuine smile, she said, "Thank you for your help. My regards to you kind wife. Good day, Mr. Horowitz."

Next she went to the mercantile and talked to Josephine Nailor, one of the Bride Brigade who'd found a job working at the mercantile.

"I need four nice potatoes and enough apples for a pie. Oh, no. I forgot to check the sugar and cinnamon. I'd better get both. I hope he has flour."

"Let me check the account." She rifled through a stack of cards until she found the one she wanted. "Yes, he bought flour on Saturday but I don't see sugar or cinnamon. Does he have milk and eggs?"

"Plenty of milk for Matthew but I don't know about eggs. I'd better take a dozen."

While Josephine gathered those for her, Angeline showed Matthew the candy. He was excited she let him choose a peppermint stick.

Josephine said, "He's so happy. Has he had candy before?"

"I have no idea. I hope his father won't be unhappy that I've given his son sweets."

Josephine laughed. "If you're making an apple pie for the preacher, I'm sure he'll forgive you anything."

"I hope so. He and Dr. Gaston have gone to the Hopkins home."

Josephine's eyes widened with alarm. "Oh, no. That sounds serious."

"I believe the eldest man of the family is dying. Would you tell Lydia I'll be late this evening? Reverend McIntyre thought he'd have to be there for most of the day."

"I'll relay the message. Nice to see you and Matthew."

Angeline firmly grasped Matthew's hand. "Come on, sticky boy. Time to go home."

Josephine hurried to the door. "Let me open that for you. Shouldn't you have us deliver your basket?"

She smiled at her friend's thoughtfulness. "Thank you, but I have a chicken in there. I'd better get it to the parsonage ice box right away."

Back at Grady's home, she unpacked her basket then cleaned up Matthew and fed him lunch. While he was napping, she prepared the pie and slid it into the oven to bake. The house filled with the tempting aroma of cinnamon and apples as she cut up the chicken.

She was grateful she didn't need to kill and strip the feathers from the chicken herself. Ugh! She'd watched cook do that. In addition to probably not being able to kill the fowl, the smell of scalded feathers was disgusting.

She and Matthew played after his nap and his apple juice and soda crackers. When the clock struck five, she stood.

"Let's make your daddy a nice supper. You can help by being a good boy. Let's put you in your high chair and you can have another of the little pieces of crust with cinnamon and sugar I baked especially for you."

He pounded the chair's serving area. "Daddy."

"That's right, Matthew. We're making something for your daddy."

With the cut up pieces in a large bowl, she seasoned them with salt and pepper. She found the lard and heated it in a large cast iron skillet. Working quickly, she beat the egg and milk together in a bowl then set out a plate of flour.

After first rolling the chicken in the flour, she dipped it in the liquid and then rolled each piece in the flour a second time. She dropped the larger pieces in the skillet first because they'd need longer to cook. She couldn't find a lid so she set a pan over the skillet.

While peeled potatoes boiled, she fried the chicken until the breaded crust was golden brown. The range's warming ledge kept the meat from cooling while she creamed the potatoes. She wouldn't make the gravy until Grady returned home for fear it would go lumpy and develop a skim. A jar of green beans from the pantry, no doubt a gift from one of the church ladies, completed the meal.

Nothing was missing but the coffee. She started that to boil and sat down to play with Matthew until his father returned.

At ten after six o'clock, Grady straggled home. He looked positively gray as he sank onto the chair nearest Matthew.

"From the look of you, the man died."

"We went ahead and buried him. Brendan Callahan at the furniture store delivered a casket this morning. All the Hopkins clan was there and wanted Zeb laid to rest in the little cemetery on their property while they were together." He raised his head and inhaled. "It was a long day but this house smells wonderful."

"Your supper is ready except for the gravy. I'll make that while you're washing your hands."

When he returned, he had removed his jacket and rolled up his sleeves. He insisted she eat with him and Matthew so she added another place at the table. She served the plates and Grady offered a blessing. While they ate, she told him about her day and he laughed at her tales of Matthew's antics.

"You should have seen him with his peppermint stick. He loved it but at least a third was on the outside. I called him 'sticky boy'. I hope you don't mind me giving him a sweet."

"No, an occasional treat is good for anyone. I try to limit his, but soda crackers are probably not that nourishing either."

"He gets a good variety of foods, though. I'd say he appears healthy and strong for his age. Today he walked a long way and didn't have to be carried."

She didn't mention her encounter of Mrs. Jackson. Why upset Grady when he'd had such a hard day. Besides, nothing he could do would change the situation.

Finally, Grady pushed away from the table. "That was the best meal I've ever eaten. The pie was a crowning touch."

"You only think that because you were tired and hungry, but you're kind to say so. I enjoyed preparing this meal for you. I knew you'd have had a hard day." She rose and carried plates to the sink.

He picked up other containers and brought them to her. She filled the dishpan with water from the range's reservoir and shaved in soap. He picked up a cup towel and dried as she washed the dishes.

She laughed at the sight of him helping her as if he did so every day.

"What's so funny?" He polished another plate.

Hoping she hadn't offended him, she plunged her hands into the water and scrubbed a bowl. "I was trying to picture my father helping my mother do anything. Truthfully, I doubt he ever did."

"You worked hard today. If you're willing to cook me a good meal and stay late to clear away the mess, why wouldn't I help?"

She didn't even try to explain to him how foreign his view was to men in the world from which she came. "You're a good man, Grady McIntyre."

"Angeline, you're a kind and caring woman. I've thought a lot about the difficult situations we both face and how we can settle them." He laid the wet towel on a rack.

Placing his hands on her shoulders, he gently turned her to face him. "You need a husband and I need a wife and Matthew needs a mother. The best thing is for you and me to wed. Say you'll marry me, Angeline."

This was her chance. Could she burden him with her problems? Thinking over how tired and forlorn he'd appeared when he came home, how much he appreciated a warm meal waiting, how he trusted her with Matthew, she realized his suggestion had merit.

She already had fallen in love with his son and suspected she was quickly falling for him. Grady was a fine man as well as handsome. He truly cared about the welfare of those in the community—not just their souls for eternity, but also their lives here and now. She'd never known a better man.

After taking a fortifying breath, she said, "If you're sure and if I can have my own room, then I agree."

A wide smile split his handsome face. "Wonderful. As for your own room, we can start out that way."

She blushed at his inference. "Who will perform the ceremony? Can you officiate at your own wedding?"

"Judge Hunter can perform the marriage. He's retired, but he's still an official in good standing."

She nodded. "You arrange the wedding and I'll be there."

"How about this Sunday afternoon? I can make the announcement in the church service and invite the congregation to return at…say three o'clock. Would that suit you?"

She thought of how rapidly her appearance was changing. "The sooner the better."

In a moment of doubt, she turned to him. "A-Are you certain you're willing to raise my baby as yours?"

He gently brushed his lips against hers as he pulled her into his arms. "How can you ask after you've been so good with Matthew? The baby you're carrying will be mine, my dear, in all the ways available. I'll cherish our child as much as I will those that follow and just as you've said you love Matthew."

She nestled her head against his chest to hide her tears and slid her arms around his waist. His heart beat strong against her ear, his warmth seeped into places that had been cold for a very long time. This was what she'd longed for. Here was not just a husband for appearance's sake, but a good man who would love and guide her child and learn to at least care for her.

Without raising her head, she asked, "And are you certain you can weather the storm your marrying a pregnant woman will create?"

His embrace tightened. "Definitely. I've come to care for you as has Matthew. We make a nice family. If I lose my position here, it won't be because of you, dear Angeline. Jackson and McGinnis were against me long before you arrived."

She raised her head to meet his lovely hazel eyes. "Don't let them win, Grady. You're important to the people here and you do a lot of good."

"I won't go unless forced to do so. I want us to raise our children right here among the people of this town. We can plant our roots deep here."

Though it was past Matthew's bedtime, Grady and his son and walked her home. "Nice to think this won't be necessary by this time next week."

"I haven't much to move. I'm sure the other girls will provide all the assistance necessary."

"I'm a willing helper, Angeline. That goes for whatever you need. Husbands and wives support and encourage one another."

"Oh, that proves even more you'll be the very husband I

always dreamed of having."

They nodded to those they met. Some smiled knowingly, others simply offered a "Good evening."

He left her at Lydia's front door. "Do I need to come ask Lydia for your hand?"

"No, but you and Matthew are welcome to come in." She peered at the boy whose head was on his father's shoulder. "He's sound asleep. The girls would squeal at our news and wake him then they'd have to play with him and get him all excited."

"You're right. I'd better leave you here and get back home and get him into bed."

"I'll see you in the morning." She slipped inside to impart her good news.

Chapter Nine

The next day, Grady talked to Judge Hunter. He was honest about Angeline's condition when he spoke of his proposal.

The Judge speared him with a scowl. "You know what Jackson and McGinnis will say about this, don't you?"

"John, there's nothing I can do that will please those two unless I scream damnation from the pulpit every Sunday and let the poor and ill fend for themselves."

The official held up his hand to ward off protest. "I wasn't suggesting you not marry this young woman. Those two dissidents want everyone to see the Bible through their warped eyes. I'd pity them if I didn't dislike them so much."

Grady allowed himself a grimace. "Doing both is possible. I've tried liking them and admit I've failed, yet I pity them for the lack of warmth in their lives. They're so bitter, they can't possibly be happy."

"You tell me when you want the ceremony and I'll be privileged to do the honors. You're a good man and I wish you the very best."

"Thank you. I'll count on you for three o'clock at the church." He shook his friend's hand and left. He walked the block to Main Street with a lighter step. Before he returned home, he had another errand.

Inside the mercantile, he greeted newly married Michael and Josephine then asked to see their wedding rings. Josephine hurried over to look on as Michael helped him.

"Don't need to ask who the bride is. I know Angeline Chandler has been caring for Matthew." Michael brought out a tray. "With Lydia's trip to get brides, I ordered a new selection."

Grady looked over the rings ranging from plain to elaborate. "I want a pretty one, but you know my salary, Michael. Show me a couple I can afford."

Josephine nudged Michael. He laughed and said, "My wife gently reminded me that since you're our minister, and a mighty fine one at that, I can let you have your choice at my cost." He pointed at one. "What do you think of this one?"

The ring wasn't all that fancy, but much nicer than the plain ones. A row of delicate leaves had been engraved on the gold band. The effect looked almost like a row of small diamonds.

"She'd like that one." When he learned the price, he exhaled with relief. "Thank you, Michael. I know you need to make a profit, and I appreciate you letting me buy this at your cost."

Josephine asked, "Are your folks coming for the wedding?"

Grady shook his head. "No, they live in Ohio. Ceremony will be Sunday afternoon. I hope you'll attend."

Michael hugged Josephine to his side. "We wouldn't miss it. Now that we're wed, we're eager for each of the Bride Brigade to find a husband. Benefits the town."

"Yes, Lydia did the community a favor when she brought her Bride Brigade here. Angeline's good for Matthew and for me. I'm looking forward to having her with us every day."

Michael leaned across the counter and winked. "Night's are mighty good too."

Josephine pretended to be shocked. "Michael Buchanan, behave yourself."

Instead of looking contrite, he laughed and slid his arm around her. "Sure glad Josephine and I are married. She's not only a good wife but she's a good business partner here. Her suggestions for new merchandise and store displays have increased profits. I'm a lucky man."

"Lucky is exactly the way I feel. Perhaps you'd do me the honor of serving as my best man." He might have had more trouble choosing between the store owner and Riley Gaston, but Michael had just let him have a discount on a ring for Angeline. That tipped the scales.

Michael beamed in pleasure. "I'd be honored."

Grady slipped the ring into the watch pocket of his waistcoat. "Thanks again for your help. I'll see you later."

After he left the store, he strolled toward home. Would he be able to weather the storm this marriage would bring? In his heart, he knew marrying Angeline was best for both of them as well as for

64

Matthew. He was convinced, yet a shadow of fear dimmed his pleasure.

***

Sunday afternoon, Angeline clasped her hands together to still their shaking.

Cassandra brushed a strand of Angeline's hair. "You'll look as pretty as any bride. If you don't stop shaking, though, I'll never get your hair styled in time."

"I'm trying. I wish I had a new dress. Grady deserves a bride in a fancy wedding dress not an old one that's been altered to accommodate my extra weight." She fought tears as she watched her friend in the mirror.

"All he cares about is you, not finery. Besides, a fancy wedding dress is a waste out here. At least for her wedding Josephine wore a dress she can use for church. That's what we all need, not something to wear once and store in a trunk."

She tugged at the jacket. "I can wear this for maybe another month. Then what will I do? What will people say? How can I answer them? Will they be mad at Grady?"

Cassandra popped her on the arm with the brush. "Good Heavens, you're making us both crazy. Stop worrying. Once you're committed to a decision, you have to remain convinced that's the best thing to do."

She met her roommate's gaze in the mirror. "You're right, Cassandra. I've chosen my path, now I'll make the best of whatever happens."

Cassandra put a last hairpin in and twirled a few loose tendrils around Angeline's face. "You look lovely." She laid the brush and comb set in the suitcase and snapped the lid shut.

A rap preceded Lydia opening the door. "Time to leave. My you do look nice, Angeline. Even though I'll miss having you here, I'm very happy for you and Grady." She handed them flowers. "I fashioned bouquets for both of you."

Angeline sniffed the combination of roses, honeysuckle, daisies, and greenery. "Thank you for this and for all you've done for me." She looked at her former roommate. "You, too, Cassandra. I'm so lucky to know both of you."

Cassandra took her arm. "Don't start saying nice things or we'll all be crying and look a mess for the ceremony. Come on, let's get going."

Lydia gestured behind her. "Adam's here to carry your belongings to the parsonage. The buggy's waiting out front."

Adam picked up the suitcases, muttering, "Sure thought she should have married Elias."

Paying his grumbling no mind, Angeline let herself be led down the stairs and to the buggy. She started to clamber up to the seat.

Behind her, Adam called, "Wait and let me help you." His hurried boot steps clomped as he caught up with them.

He drove Lydia, Cassandra, and her. The other girls strolled chattering and laughing and waved as the buggy passed. She saw Grady's buggy parked beside his home.

At the parsonage, Adam helped her to the ground. "You wait inside the house. Let's set your cases in there then I'll go check to see if folks are seated."

Lydia hugged Angeline. "I'll go with Adam so I can find a place."

Angeline and Cassandra stood in the parlor waiting for the sheriff to return.

Angeline wandered to the window to count the number of buggies. "I hope enough people showed up to support Grady that he won't feel slighted."

"I'm sure they have. What else are they going to do on Sunday afternoon?" Cassandra peered around the room. "Not a bad home, is it? You should be happy here." She wandered into other rooms.

Angeline didn't mind her friend's curiosity. If she weren't so nervous, she would have given Cassandra a proper tour. Instead, she set her cases in the bedroom and then paced the small parlor.

Adam's reappearance relieved her mind. "You ready to get hitched?"

"I am. Thank you for agreeing to walk me down the aisle. I'm so nervous I'm not sure I'd be able to stand on my own."

Cassandra hurried to walk with them and closed the door as they left the parsonage.

"Don't worry about a thing, Miss Chandler." He chuckled. "Say, that's the last time you'll hear anyone call you that."

That was fine with her. Chandler had only unhappy memories associated with it. She'd be glad to exchange her overbearing father's surname for that of a kind, caring man.

Inside the church, Angeline was surprised and relieved the sanctuary was filled. Mrs. Ramirez had charge of Matthew. At the front, Grady stood with Michael Buchanan and Judge Hunter. Cassandra walked in front of her as her maid of honor.

When Grady spotted her, his face lit with happiness. That fact alone gave Angeline the encouragement she needed to walk proudly down the aisle. He was happy to see her, what else could matter?

When she drew even with Mrs. Ramirez at the end of a pew, Matthew reached up his arms and cried, "Angel. Want my Angel."

He got away from Mrs. Ramirez and scrambled toward her. She smiled at the woman and held out her hand. Matthew walked the rest of the way with her.

At the front, Adam left her with Grady then sat beside Lydia. Adam's stage whisper carried, "Whew, I feel like a parent giving up a daughter."

A murmur of chuckles rippled from those who had heard.

Judge Hunter's dignified manner commanded attention as he conducted the ceremony. She handed her bouquet to Cassandra and slid her free hand into Grady's. She wanted to remember every word of the service, but all she could focus on was Grady's smile and his strong hand holding hers and the little boy with them.

After their vows, Judge Hunter said, "You may kiss the bride."

Grady's hazel eyes sparkled and he gently brushed his lips across hers. She held on to him and must have released Matthew's hand.

"Daddy. Angel. Me a kiss." She looked down to see Matthew with his arms reaching to be lifted.

Grady lifted his son and held him with one arm. The other, he placed around her. She leaned over to kiss Matthew.

The judge announced, "May I present Mr. and Mrs. McIntyre. And Matthew."

Chuckles again resounded in the congregation. Grady led her from the church to his buggy. Behind them, she heard Lydia invite everyone to her home for a reception.

"We'll have to hurry to arrive before the others." Grady set his son on the seat then lifted her up. He hurried around to the other side and hopped onto the seat.

She held on to Matthew so he wouldn't fall and Grady flicked the reins to set the buggy skimming along the road.

"I still can't believe we had this lovely wedding and we're being given a reception. I'm overjoyed, Grady. I can't ever remember being this happy."

He grinned. "I'm in high spirits myself. We're going to share a wonderful life here." He parked in front of Lydia's, set the brake, and hopped to the ground. Once he'd lifted her down, he carried Matthew and they made their way to the house.

Mrs. Greenberg opened the door. "I'm sorry I had to miss your ceremony, dear, but someone had to be here to see to last minute details. Moira missed the other wedding so this was my turn to hold things together."

Angeline asked, "Are we to go upstairs to the ballroom or wait here?"

The kindly maid pointed upward. "You folks go right on up and stand where the Buchanans did. You'll see everything's ready but the crowd and they'll be here soon enough."

They hurried because they heard the chatter of voices approaching. When they were inside the ballroom, they took their places near the doorway ready to greet everyone who entered.

Matthew stared at the table laden with a large cake, several small ones, and plates of cookies. A large punchbowl sat at one end.

Her son pointed and tried to get down from his father's arms. "Let's go eat."

Angeline raced to the table and grabbed a couple of cookies. She returned to stand by Grady as the first people came to greet them. Silently handing her new son a cookie, she was left wondering what to do with the extra one. Quickly, she slid the other into Grady's pocket in case Matthew needed a refill before they were free of the line.

She was shocked to see people place gifts on a table near the refreshments. Of course she knew they were because her husband was the minister, but she was thrilled.

Ophelia and Cassandra tried to coax Matthew away from Grady and her.

The little the boy scrunched up his face to cry. "Want Angel and Daddy."

She smiled at her friends. "Thank you, but we'll keep him with us."

Between greeting people, Angeline leaned toward Grady. "Most people have come for the reception."

He whispered, "Even the Jackson and McGinnis couples are here. They're even more cheerful than normal."

"Maybe they're softening toward you."

He shook his head. "Not likely but that's a nice thought."

Mrs. Ramirez reached for Matthew. "Perhaps this fine boy will let me entertain him for a while. Doreen will be so upset she's missed your wedding." She led Matthew over to a chair and helped him sit beside her. The child watched Grady and her but he seemed content to sit beside the woman who had helped care for him for a large part of his life.

Grady led her to the refreshment table. "I had to wake him from his nap. Keep your fingers crossed."

Lydia greeted them. "We saved the main cake for you to cut. After another thirty minutes, give Lola Ramirez a signal and she'll meet you at the stairs with Matthew. Forgive me when you see your buggy, but Adam and Riley just couldn't resist decorating it."

Grady chuckled. "I'd have felt slighted if they had."

They cut the cake and then served themselves and accepted punch from Lorraine, who served the drink to those who wanted some. Prudence attended a large coffee urn. Other girls appeared to be occupied making trips back and forth to the kitchen for refills of both beverages and to carry used plates and cups.

Angeline accepted refreshment from Lorraine. "I wonder how many of those punch cups Lydia has?"

Lorraine raised her eyebrows. "I asked before the ball. She has three hundred. We used them all, People kept setting theirs down and then getting a fresh one. I remember you were helping wash them like mad."

Lydia approached Angeline and Grady. "Because some people don't approve of dancing on Sunday, we won't have dancing." She looked toward Harlie Jackson. "I didn't want to create a problem for you."

Grady's smile didn't reach his eyes. "To my mind, we shouldn't do anything on any other day we'd be ashamed to do on Sunday, but I appreciate your tact. This is the Lord's day."

Finally, they'd stayed long enough to please everyone. They waved goodbye and went downstairs. Many people followed, laughing and calling to them. Outside, the buggy was bedecked with bows and a sign on back that said "Just married". Another proclaimed "Leg

Shackled" and a third said "Grady's new ball and chain"

As they drove away, Grady said, "At least they don't give shivarees. Well, they haven't since I've lived here. I certainly hope they don't start with us"

"I don't know what that is."

He shrugged and looked ahead. "For instance, if they were going to give us one, men would parade around the house all night banging on pans to make noise and keep us awake, hoping to interfere with our wedding night. In some places, they even kidnap the bride and toss the groom in jail. Or toss them both in the horse tank. Or they might have snuck into the house to do things like tie cowbells to the bed springs, stupid things like that."

Angeline clasped Matthew to her. "I can't believe something like what would be allowed in this day and time. That sounds uncivilized and horrible,"

Grady shrugged. "To some, it's fun. I suspect never to the bride and groom. Not the sort of thing I consider humorous."

She shivered at the thought. "I'd think to a less forgiving person, a gun might be involved to halt that type of so-called fun. Oh, I guess I shouldn't think like that since I'm now a minister's wife."

He sent her a serious look. "Ministers are just people, Angeline. We have the same needs and desires others do."

"I wasn't deifying you, Grady. But you do set an example for the community. In spite of my condition, I want to do the same."

"You already do, my dear." He set the brake and climbed down. "Fabian promised to take the horse and buggy back to the livery for us."

"Everyone has been so kind today." She handed him their sleepy boy. "He's had a busy day. By the way, there's a cookie still in your pocket."

He laughed. "Now I remember. When you didn't know what to do with the second cookie, you stashed the thing in my jacket."

Inside the house, she lit a lamp against falling dusk. This cozy house was her home. Her heart swelled with gratitude. Her baby would be welcomed to a safe place with a loving father.

"Let me make Matthew and you supper. I hope cookies didn't spoil his appetite." She pulled an apron over her head and tied the strings behind her.

"No, surely there's something we can snack on so there's no

need to cook." He opened the ice box.

With a triumphant smile, he removed the wax paper from a plate of last night's fried chicken. "Here's the perfect thing."

He'd had to visit someone out in the county on Saturday, so she'd cooked his favorite dinner again. "You've had fried chicken twice this week. I don't think we need it again."

His grin reminded her of his son's mischievous face. "Too late." He set the plate on the table and helped Matthew into his high chair.

The little boy's face brightened and he reached for the dish, which Grady had cleverly placed out of the child's reach. "Chicken goes cluck cluck. Let's eat."

"All right. You men win." She felt inside of the ice box to judge the temperature. Jo Jo had delivered ice only yesterday, so the food was nice and cool.

She picked up the milk container. "I'll pour us milk and we can fill in with last night's potato salad and deviled eggs. We'll have an indoor picnic."

Angeline set the table but her mind was consumed by worry. Would Grady remember his promise to let her have a private bedroom? Only minutes ago, he'd mentioned that he was a man. She saw the passion in his eyes and knew he wanted to consummate their marriage.

Memories of the painful and humiliating experience which ended her in this predicament haunted her. The animalistic behavior of the man who'd promised to love her forever. Pain of his assault. Horace's disregard for her discomfort and embarrassment. She forced herself not to shudder at her recollection.

Knowing Grady would never act in such a hurtful way didn't reassure her as much as she'd hoped. He was a man worthy of her trust. She had to stop these disturbing thoughts before they showed in her face and movement. Otherwise, she was likely to hurt her kind husband's feelings.

She forced a smile for her groom. "You're very thoughtful to settle for a cold meal of leftovers."

"You know I love your cooking, but a bride shouldn't have to prepare her wedding supper. I'm surprised Mrs. Murphy didn't bring us something."

"She and Lydia wanted to, but I selfishly declined so there

would be just our family, with no intrusion of any kind after the reception. I hope that's all right. I should have asked you."

His gaze captured hers. "Angeline, hearing you say 'our family' in that way pleases me more than you could know. I'm grateful you think of us that way, for so do I."

Together, they tidied the kitchen and put Matthew to bed. Her nervousness increased.

At what would be her door, Grady placed his hands at her waist. "I haven't forgotten you asked for your own room, my dear. I'll sleep on the bed near Matthew. Promise me that when you're ready to accept me as your husband in every way, you'll tell me."

"But I'm...surely we couldn't...have relations now. Doing so would cause me to lose the baby."

His kindly hazel eyes appeared to memorize her features. "You're wrong on that score, my dear." He caressed her face. "Don't look alarmed. I'm not going back on my word."

Her heartbeat accelerated. She was grateful for this man as her husband. "I never thought you would. I'll think about us, Grady. I don't want you to be sorry we're wed."

"I'm glad you're my wife, Angeline, and I hope soon to hold you in my arms while we sleep. In the meantime, I believe a husband is allowed to kiss his wife goodnight."

She titled her face to meet his mouth. The sweet sensation his lips created spiraled through her and settled in her core. His kiss deepened and he pulled her close. As she settled against him, a startling movement in her stomach made her gasp.

She pulled away and clutched her abdomen. "What was that? I thought my stomach moved. Did you feel anything?"

He tilted her chin to meet his gaze. "That was the baby kicking. Is this the first time you've felt him or her moving?"

"Ohhh, you mean she's moving inside me? I never knew I'd feel her. This is a miracle. And on our wedding day."

"From now on until birth, you'll feel the movements grow stronger."

"Grady, I'm so ignorant of what to expect. Girls aren't told what will happen as their bodies change. I'm lucky you know what's supposed to happen and when."

"Have you been to see Riley? That's Dr. Gaston."

"No. I-I didn't want anyone to know about the baby until

someone proposed. Except for a month of morning nausea, I've felt fine." Only if she didn't count the endless panic and worry.

"Tomorrow, see Riley to be certain everything is as it should be. He'll be able to explain things to you if you have questions."

"If you insist, but I'd really prefer to wait."

"Angeline, if I guessed, others must have, especially a doctor."

Her shoulders slumped. Why had she been so naïve as to think she could hide her condition? "You're right. I'll go tomorrow."

He pulled her back into his arms and kissed her hair. "Don't worry, my dear. We're together and that's the most important thing."

"Thank you, Grady, for all you've done for me. Goodnight."

"Goodnight, my dear."

In her room, she held her hand up to gaze at her wedding band again. A sign of infinite love and devotion as she hoped their marriage would become. And Grady had chosen one with a beautiful decorative vine circling. The design sparkled like tiny diamonds. Once again she gave thanks for her wonderful husband and son.

Chapter Ten

Angeline loved her new life. Frequently, Grady took her and Matthew with him on morning calls to visit the elderly. Today, Matthew was not his usual cheerful self, but no one appeared to mind. They were on a call to Mrs. Eppes when the room darkened.

Their hostess asked, "Did a cloud come up? 'Pears to me things got darker."

Grady looked out the window. "Looks as if we're in for a rainstorm. If you'll excuse us, Mrs. Eppes, I think I'd better get my wife and son home."

"There was nothing in the almanac about this. Hurry on, but come again soon." She struggled to stand.

Angeline leaned down and hugged her. "Don't get up, Mrs. Eppes. We'll see ourselves out. I've put things away in the kitchen, but if you wish I'll make you a bite to eat while we're here."

"No, you get that fine boy home. Mrs. Querado comes at noon."

Grady carried Matthew and they hurried the four blocks toward the parsonage. By the time they were a few houses away from Mrs. Eppes', the wind swirled dust devils down the street. Sand stung her skin and she tried to shield Matthew with her parasol. At the corner, fat raindrops splattered them.

Grady put Matthew on the ground while he took off his jacket and wrapped it around the little boy then scooped him into his arms again. He placed a hand at her elbow. "Walk as fast as you can without falling, my dear. We can't have you catching cold."

"Oh, I hope the downpour doesn't ruin our flowers."

Thunder rumbled and the heavens opened. Her flimsy parasol was useless against the wind and rain blowing horizontally at them. She struggled against the gusts until they turned onto the drive to the church. They were drenched by the time they reached the parsonage.

Inside, she removed her sodden hat and pushed her hair from her face. "Guess we should have waited at Mrs. Eppes'." She picked up a towel and handed it to Grady and set to work drying a sobbing Matthew with another.

"It may rain all day. Poor, Matthew, the jacket didn't help much, did it?"

"At least some." She knelt in front of the boy. "There, now, Matthew. No need to cry, good boy. Give Angeline a smile. Daddy got us home just fine. Now we'll be dry and warm."

Grady carried his son toward the bedroom. "I'll get us both into dry clothes and you do the same for yourself."

She changed clothes quickly and hurried into the kitchen to get a mid-day meal on the table. When her men rejoined her, Matthew no longer cried but he rubbed his eyes.

She buttered a piece of bread and handed it to the boy. "How about a snack?"

Matthew pulled at the bread but ate only a few bites.

She poured three glasses of milk and set them on the table.

Grady helped his sleepy son with a drink then checked his pocket watch. "He's not usually so sleepy yet."

"You'd think that rain would have woke him more. He might be still cold from the downpour. I'll heat the stew from yesterday so he can get something warm into his tummy."

They quickly consumed their hearty soup with her feeding Matthew between her own spoons full.

She cajoled her son into a smile. "There's my happy boy."

After standing, she refilled Grady's bowl. "You eat while I put our boy down for his nap." She lifted Matthew and carried him. After making sure he'd used his potty, she put him into his crib. Though it was summer, she covered him with a light blanket to ward off a chill from the change in weather.

"He dropped right off to sleep." She rejoined him at the table and found a full bowl at her place.

Grady smiled at her. "I served you more of the stew. Then I think you should have a nap too. I might even have one. I don't think we'll have callers in this weather."

"I hope not, for that would indicate an emergency."

Later that afternoon, Angeline noticed that Matthew's nose was runny and touched his forehead. "Grady, he feels feverish. I think he caught cold in the rain, although maybe he was already feeling bad. Remember how sleepy he was?"

"You have a point. If he was coming down with something, getting wet would make it worse." Grady knelt beside Matthew's high chair. "Do you feel bad, son? Does something hurt?"

"Drink, Daddy."

"Of course. Let me get you some cool water." He rose and pumped a pitcher of water then poured some into a small glass for his son. "I've heard giving milk to feverish patients is a bad idea."

Matthew drank all of the water. "Hurts here." He held his throat.

"Poor baby. Should you go get the doctor?"

"There's nothing Riley can do for a cold. Chicken soup is good for fever and cold. My mom used to make it for us with a little garlic, a few slices of carrots, spices, and a tiny bit of onion."

She reached for his slicker which hung on a peg by the kitchen door. "I'll go to Mr. Horowitz's and get a couple of fryers—one for soup and one to fry for you."

He caught her hand to stop her. "You will not, my dear. All we need is for you to hurry and slip on the wet ground. I'll go since I believe he needs the soup."

"I'm going to learn to can so I can keep things like that on hand." The thought gave her an idea. "Wait, let me check the larder and see if one of the congregation might have brought you some in the past." She opened the pantry and checked jars the ladies of the town had brought.

Grady picked up Matthew, who had become fussy, rare behavior for the boy.

She grasped a quart jar gratefully and clutched it to her. "What a blessing Martha Granger is for giving you two of these! We can stay dry and feed Matthew chicken soup for his supper."

Soothing his son, Grady paced the kitchen. "I remember she brought those when I had a cold this winter. Mrs. Murphy brought a large pan of warm soup so I shoved the jars back in the pantry to save for another day and promptly forgot about them."

She opened the jar and poured the contents into a sauce pan. "We can benefit from a bowl, since we were drenched."

"Don't know where he caught his cold. He's always been healthy."

After supper, they put their son to bed but Matthew didn't want to sleep. He cried, which only made him more stopped up and uncomfortable.

"You stay with him, Grady while I tidy up the kitchen." She fetched the pitcher of water and glass from the kitchen. "I think he should drink as much water as possible, even if it means changing him and his sheets during the night."

"I'll put his old soakers on him just in case, not that they'll keep him dry. Might save the bed is all they're good for."

She hurried into the kitchen and tidied as quickly as she could. She'd cared for her neighbor's children, but not when they were ill. Having her boy sick worried her. What could she do to make him well? To make him more comfortable?

Grady held Matthew on his shoulder and rubbed his back. The little boy dropped off to sleep but waked when Grady tried to put him in his bed. "Go to bed, my dear. I'll watch him. If he gets more congested, I'll take him to the kitchen and make a steam tent with the kettle."

She stood wringing her hands. "I need to learn these things so I can care for him. I sort of remember having croup and Mama putting a sheet over my head and making me breathe the kettle's steam. I didn't like it because it was hot."

"I'll wager Matthew won't like it, either, but it helps."

Relieved to have something constructive to do for the little boy, she said, "I'll put the kettle on to boil and get a sheet. We can try now and maybe he'll sleep better."

When they had finished and the cranky boy was asleep in his crib, Angeline folded the sheet and laid it on a chair in case they needed it again.

"Go on to bed, my dear. I'll call you if he wakes and I need help with him."

She shook her head and hugged her arms. "I can't sleep while you're keeping watch."

After placing an arm around her shoulders, he said, "Remember you're sleeping for two. You have to keep our baby healthy."

Tears welled in her eyes. "Oh, Grady, you are the kindest, best husband in the entire world."

He offered a sad smile and shook his finger at her. "No, no, no crying. One fretful member of the McIntyre household is all I can handle. Off to bed with you now."

Angeline was certain she wouldn't be able to close her eyes as she readied for bed. When she crawled between the sheets, she was exhausted. She kept her ear tuned to the sounds in the next room but soon fell asleep.

The next morning, Grady carried Matthew into the kitchen for breakfast. "He seems a little better this morning." Or, was that wishful thinking on his part?

Angeline was at the range when they entered. She came to kiss Matthew but offered Grady only a grin. As much as he enjoyed her winsome smile, he wondered if the time would come when she would greet him with a kiss. He longed for them to be married in every way and to share closeness that intimacy created.

She smoothed a hand over Matthew's hair. "I have oatmeal ready."

While she bustled about ladling the warm cereal into bowls, Grady secured his son in the high chair and scooted him up to the table.

After the blessing, he picked up his spoon and added sugar to his bowl then milk. "I have an appointment with Harlie Jackson this morning. Hate to leave you on your own with a sick boy, but I need to show up for this meeting."

"Mothers take care of sick children on their own all the time." She met his gaze, a worried frown on her pretty face. "What does Mr. Jackson want?"

He took a sip of coffee before he answered, "No idea, but I'm sure it's not to tell me I'm doing a great job. He'll have a burr under his saddle about something."

With a savage jab of her spoon, she attacked her oatmeal as if she were battling Jackson. "I wish he'd change his attitude. You do a wonderful job preaching and caring for the community whether they attend church or not."

Most of his congregation members were congenial and approving of his ministry. "That's one of his complaints." He exhaled in frustration. "I'll not back down on the way I'm ministering."

Later, as he walked toward the Jackson home, he worried about Harlie Jackson and his yes-man, Ulys McGinnis. They had been more critical of late. In spite of his conviction that he was faithful to a

Biblical ministry, he dreaded the meeting today.

When Lizzie Jackson showed him into the parlor, he saw that Ulys McGinnis was also present. He took the seat Harlie indicated.

But he wished he were anywhere but here. "Harlie, Ulys, how are you today?"

Appearing even more stern than usual, Harlie fixed him with a glare. "Let's get right to the point of why we asked you here. We're concerned about your wife."

He'd been expecting something like this, but he had no intention of letting anyone slander her. "Angeline? She's a lovely woman and a good wife and mother to Matthew. She also kindly visits members of the congregation and reads to some of the older ladies."

Harlie stabbed a finger at him. "She looks as if she's expecting a baby and is far enough along she must have conceived before she set foot in Tarnation."

"And why does that concern you? As her husband, surely I'm the only one who has a right to have an opinion on that subject."

Ulys leaned forward. "She was introduced to us as single, not as a widow. We don't think a fallen woman is fit to be in church."

Grady hated this but he'd try to nip it in the bud before dissension spread. "You believe each of our members has to be perfect?"

Harlie appeared taken aback, but by no means stumped. "Of course not, but you can't expect respectable people to allow a tarnished woman in their midst. Bad enough you hold a service for the saloon girls, but now you've married one."

Grady's blood boiled. "You will not speak about my wife in that way. For your information, she is an exceptionally good and compassionate woman. One mistake which was not of her choice should not condemn a person for life."

Ulys shook his head. "You're either respectable or you're not. If you fall short, then you don't belong in our church."

Grady wished he weren't against brawling. He'd love to smack these men's heads together. "That attitude is what keeps many saloon girls from being able to reform and leave that life. You two are so busy judging people you forget what church is about. Have you read the Bible? Have you listened to any of my sermons?"

Harlie leapt to his feet. "I've heard that pap you feed us from the pulpit. I've read the Bible too. Women like your wife would have been stoned." He appeared surprised he was standing and reclaimed his chair.

As calmly as he could manage, Grady said, "No, they wouldn't. Don't you remember our Lord asking who is blameless to cast the first stone? Are you perfect, Harlie?" He turned to the other man. "And you Ulys, have you never made a mistake?"

Grady stood. "I've other calls to make, gentlemen. There is nothing to be gained by continuing at cross purposes. This discussion is ended."

Harlie narrowed his eyes. "You may think it is, preacher, but you haven't heard the last of this by any means."

Picking up his hat, Grady said, "Good day."

He was so angry his insides shook. He hoped he appeared calmer than that, but he couldn't have contained his anger any longer if he'd continued listening to those two bigots. Respectable indeed. No one in town liked them because of their tendency to look down on others.

On his way back to the parsonage, he stopped in at the mercantile. Fortunately, he'd come at a time when there were no other customers.

Michael stood at the counter talking with Josephine. "Hey, Grady. You look a mite upset."

He exhaled slowly, searching for calm. "Just came from the Jackson home where I met with Harlie and Ulys."

Michael and Josephine exchanged knowing looks. "No wonder you're riled. Why don't you come in the back and have a seat for a bit? Haven't had a chance to talk to you in a while."

Nodding at Josephine, Grady followed the other man to the little table and two chairs in the storeroom. He took a seat, still quaking inside.

Michael tilted back in his chair. "Had a go at you about your wife, did they?"

Surprised, he glanced up. "How did you know?"

"You usually let their complaints roll off you but you appear so angry you may explode."

He gave a derisive laugh. "I almost did at that. I had to leave the Jackson home or hit either Harlie or Ulys or both." He ran a hand across his face. "You know I'm against brawling on principle, but I can understand how a man can lose control and light into someone."

"Don't let them get to you. Two malcontents out of the whole county is a pretty good ratio of approval. Don't know anyone else with that rating. You know, hard as we try to run a good store, we get complaints too."

He shook his head, worry settling on his shoulders like a mantle. "They make enough noise and other people will listen. Followers are easily persuaded to change their minds."

Michael leaned forward to rest his arms on the table. "I guess they took you to task because Angeline's expecting. Who better than a minister to have married her? Besides, you're good together. She was doing your work in the community on her own before she married you."

"You're right on both counts. They want to condemn her because she was expecting when she came here. And she is a kind woman who genuinely cares about people."

"Don't have to tell me. People come in here and sing her praises. One of them is Riley because your wife convinced several of his patients to take medicine he prescribed and are now feeling better. She accomplished in a few visits what he hadn't been able to in months."

Grady smiled for the first time since he'd left home after breakfast. "She reads to people who no longer see well and does their mending. She brings cheer wherever she goes. One mistake trusting a callous man who attacked and deserted her doesn't define who she is."

Michael slapped a hand on the table. "She's a fine woman that Josephine and I are proud to call our friend. You can tell she loves Matthew, too. You chose well, my friend."

Feeling better, he rubbed a hand across his face, wishing he could scrub away Harlie and Ulys as easily. "Thanks for letting me blow off steam. I owe you."

The store owner shrugged away his comment. "What are friends for?"

He scraped back his chair and stood. "Well, how about selling me a length of green ribbon and three peppermint sticks?"

Chapter Eleven

When Grady left the store, he was in a much better frame of mind. After seven years as a minister, he knew better than to let a couple of naysayers get under his skin. Nothing he could do or say would please everyone in the congregation, and those who were unhappy were usually eager to let him know. When it came to Angeline, though, apparently he had a lower tolerance level.

That thought created questions in his head. He cared for her, but perhaps he was growing more than just fond of her. Remembering his first wife, Georgia, he wondered if he was being unfaithful.

Funny how that thought sprang into his mind. Georgia was gone and Angeline was here. How could caring for Angeline be wronging Georgia? If he were counseling someone with this dilemma, he would tell the person how destructive that line of thought could be to the new relationship.

Georgia still resided in his heart, but there was plenty of room for Angeline, Matthew, and any children that came along, including the baby Angeline now carried. For his sake, he hoped the baby looked like her. He'd love the child regardless of appearances, but he would enjoy having a miniature copy of his wife.

He stopped by Riley's office but the doctor was out. A large blackboard hung on the wall. The doctor had written "Seeing Mrs. Oliver north of town."

On the same blackboard left, Grady wrote a note. "*Matthew McIntyre sick. Stop by when you can.*"

By the time he reached home, he'd recovered his composure and hoped to keep the upsetting visit with Harlie and Ulys from his thoughts.

When he entered the kitchen, Angeline balanced a fussy Matthew on her hip. "There's Daddy."

Her eyes held question he wanted to answer without alarming

her. He took his son from her. "How's our boy? I brought us a treat."

She accepted the small package he handed her. "What's this? Surely it's not from the Jacksons?" She untied the string and pulled away the brown paper.

"I splurged and bought us all a sweet and you a tiny gift."

A sweet smile appeared on her face. "A ribbon to wear with my green skirt and top. How thoughtful of you, Grady." She held a peppermint stick out to their son. "And I'll bet Matthew remembers what this is."

"Candy." Matthew reached for the sweet.

Grady had no desire to wear sticky sugar on his clothes and set his son in the high chair. "He's still as congested."

"I made a steam tent again, but I should have waited for you. He hates it and holding him and the sheet without your help is almost too much for me."

"I'm not going out again today. After we have dinner, I'll stay here and work on my sermon for tomorrow so I'll be handy whenever you need me."

"I thought he was better after the steam but the effect didn't last long. I'll bet the sweet will make his throat feel better."

"But he always gets worse about sundown. This is an unusual time of year for croup. I left a note for Riley to come by when he can, but he's north of town seeing a patient."

Angeline sat at the table and gave their son a drink of water. "What if Matthew isn't better by tomorrow?"

"I don't think he should go out, my dear. Do you mind staying here with him instead of going to church?"

She stared at him with hurt showing in her wide eyes. "How can you ask? Of course I'll stay home with him. I was worried about not showing up to church after you being called on the carpet by Mr. Jackson."

He pulled her into his embrace and tucked her head under his chin. "I meant no slight. You shouldn't worry about Jackson or McGinnis. They're never going to be happy so best not waste effort giving them a thought."

She leaned against him. "I can't help disliking them, Grady. I'm not proud of that, but I've tried and simply can't."

He savored having her in his arms. "You'd be a saint if you could. As Christians we're to love everyone, but that doesn't mean we have to enjoy them. I'll wager not many people in Tarnation like either of those couples."

She pulled away and busied herself making a pie for dinner.

***

Almost in tears from worry, Angeline walked the floor with Matthew until Grady returned from the church service. She'd almost hurried to the church with the boy to seek help from more experienced mothers or the doctor. He fussed if she put him down, so she'd held him all morning, bathing his face with a cold cloth and feeding him cool water.

Grady came through the door and took off his jacket before he took his son from her. "People asked about you and sent prayers and good wishes for both you and Matthew. Most expressed hope neither of us caught our boy's cold. Riley wasn't there this morning but I hope he'll return to town soon."

She set about preparing dinner. "Matthew's much worse. I'm sure of it."

"If Riley doesn't return by evening, I'll ask one of the older women in town for advice. I'm sure Riley will drop in as soon as he can." He tried to sound calm, but she knew he was as worried as she was.

By the time Riley arrived about four, Matthew gasped for breath.

Riley pumped water in the sink and washed his hands with lye soap. "Sorry I had to stay all night at the Olivers. Thought for a while I'd have to bring her to town with me."

Angeline didn't know the family but asked, "Is she going to be all right?"

"Eventually, but she's mighty sick. Talked her husband out of sending for me until she was too bad to protest. Now, let's check this big boy."

Usually a happy child, Matthew tried to turn away from the doctor. Riley didn't appear to let a fussy child interfere with his examination. After listening to the boy's lungs, he frowned.

"What have you done to ease his breathing?"

Grady explained about the rainstorm and everything they'd done to try to help Matthew.

"You've done the right things, but he has pneumonia. He must already have been getting sick when the rain caught you."

His diagnosis set fear gnawing at her insides. Pneumonia was deadly. She held Matthew's little hand in hers. "He's so small. Tell us what to do."

Grady put his hand at her back as if to reassure her. Or was he as frightened as she was?

Riley appeared exhausted but he smiled. "I'll stay a while and help."

Grady asked, "When did you sleep last?"

The doctor shrugged as if his sleep were unimportant. "A few hours last night and in the buggy coming home. Horse knows the way to town."

He dug into his medical bag and brought out a small green bottle. "This is menthol. Put a spoonful in the kettle when you make the steam tent and this will open him up more. Don't worry, Angeline, breathing the mix won't hurt you or your baby."

Riley produced a brown bottle. "This is a blend I concoct myself for asthma and chest complaints. Give him half a spoonful every hour until his breathing eases then change to every four hours. He won't like the taste, but he needs to swallow every drop."

Holding up a blue bottle, he said. "This will reduce the fever and his achiness, but at his age you can't give him much. Put four drops in a cup of water and get him to drink all of it every four hours until his fever breaks." He opened an envelope of labels and took out a pencil. He pasted the strip of paper with the instructions on each container.

"We'll follow your instructions."

They gave the boy the two concoctions and then made a steam tent. The mentholated steam plus the other medicines didn't please Matthew.

After the tent, Angeline cried, "Thank Heavens, he's breathing easier. Oh, Matthew baby, you're better."

Grady clutched Matthew to him. "Can't thank you enough, Riley. We didn't know what else to try. You go on home and get some sleep. Looks like Matthew might be able to do the same."

"As a last resort, you can make a sugar tit. Um, sorry if that offends you, Angeline, but that's what it's called. You take a small square of clean white cloth and fill it with raw sugar and tie a string to bind the sugar inside a nipple-like pouch. Drop on barely enough whiskey to moisten the sugar and then let him suck on the bag. I don't like to give babies spirits, but crying increases his congestion. A small amount of liquor on the sugar won't hurt him and will help pacify his fussing."

Cradling Matthew on his left side, Grady extended his right hand to the doctor. "Thanks, Riley. You're a good friend as well as a good doctor."

Clasping Grady's hand, Riley shook it. "You know I'm fond of your son, but tending the sick is my job."

Angeline hugged the doctor. "Thank you for coming before you got the rest you need, Riley." Surprised at her forwardness, she stepped back and her face heated with embarrassment.

The doctor grinned at her, mirth shining from his tired eyes. "Much nicer than a handshake." He looked at Grady. "If you follow my instructions and his fever breaks, he'll be all right. But let me know immediately if he gets worse."

"We will. Go catch up on your sleep."

When the doctor had gone, Angeline and Grady followed the physician's instructions precisely.

About midnight, Grady said, "You need your sleep. He's breathing better. Go to bed and if he gets worse, I'll call you to watch while I go for Riley."

"How could I rest when our poor little boy is gasping for breath?" She ran a hand over the child's fevered brow.

Grady encouraged Matthew to drink more water from his cup. "You can't endanger yourself or our baby. Please, if you won't go to your room, lie down on my bed. Then you can hear him, but at least you'll be off your feet and resting."

She hated to give in to weakness, but her ankles were swollen and her back hurt from carrying Matthew so long. "I suppose you're right. I'll just rest and get my feet up. Then we can take turns and you rest while I hold him."

She took off her shoes and crawled onto the bed. Ah, aching in her back and legs eased. Curled on her side, she watched Grady and their son. What a wonderful father Grady was.

Once again, she gave thanks she'd married this fine man.

When next she became aware, she was curled with her head on Grady's shoulder. His arm rested across her just below her breasts. Contentment engulfed her. This must be what truly being married was like. Slowly, she moved her head to see if he slept.

He smiled at her and tightened his embrace. "Great way to wake up. I could get used to this." He wouldn't be smiling unless their son had improved.

She whispered, "Matthew's better?"

"His fever broke and he's breathing easier. I put him in his bed and joined you. He hasn't fussed for about three hours."

Alarm shot through her. "You're sure he's—"

"He's breathing. I've checked. Relax and let me hold you for a while longer."

"I should get our breakfast."

"I hope you don't mind but I felt our baby kick again. Amazing what a miracle a growing infant is. A confirmation of a planned life cycle."

"I'm not sorry I'll have this baby, Grady, not now that you've taken me in and accepted the child. Marrying you was the best day of my life."

He kissed her hair. "We'll have many good days. Occasionally bad ones, too, because that's the way the world works. Good ones will outweigh the bad."

Reluctant to leave his arms, she sat up. "The way nature works is that expectant mothers have to visit the privy frequently. When I come back in, I'll prepare breakfast."

Hurrying to the privy, she relived being in his arms. How different he was from Horace, thank Heavens. She knew Grady wanted them to sleep in the same bed and to have relations, but he didn't press her.

She suspected allowing her husband to share her body would be different than with Horace. How could she have trusted Horace Brady? Her father thought highly of him, and that should have been a clue he was not right for her.

Her father's wealth was a draw for those seeking marriage to a woman who'd inherit a fortune. Not that she would now, for she was certain her father would leave his money to charity rather than let her have a cent. Thinking about her life in Missouri was pointless and depressing. She should concentrate on being a good wife for the wonderful man who'd married her.

She vowed that the next time he mentioned them sharing a bed, she'd agree.

By Wednesday, Matthew was his normal self, happily playing

with his toys. For a couple of weeks life ran smoothly and Angeline was happier than she'd ever been in her life.

One morning, Lydia came to call. "You're looking happy when I see you at church, but I haven't had a chance to talk to you privately."

Angeline poured hot water into the teapot. While it steeped, she sliced two pieces of applesauce cake. "I never dreamed I could be so content. Thank you so much for rescuing me so I could meet Grady and have this life."

Lydia picked up her fork and cut a dainty bite of her dessert. "You meeting and marrying someone was the goal, wasn't it? I'm glad you and Grady are finding your way."

Angeline poured milk into her cup and added tea. "I sense there's more, Lydia. What's wrong?"

As if reluctant, Lydia confessed, "I've heard rumors in town that someone is trying to get Grady ousted as minister. I can imagine who's behind this, but I have no proof. Grady needs to be warned, though."

Bitterness swelled in Angeline and sharpened her reply. "Harlie Jackson and Ulys McGinnis threatened him a few weeks ago. They think he's too soft and liberal in his ministry."

Lydia agreed, "There's no telling what those two are up to, but they're talking to everyone in the community. I doubt they can cause Grady to lose his job, but they can make his life unpleasant."

Angeline stabbed a bite of cake. "They've already done that, but from what you say, they're mounting a campaign. I'll warn him when he comes in from calling on the Olivers."

"Oh, yes, I heard she's been ill. I don't know the family, but I'm glad to hear she's recovering."

"Yes, but they aren't members of this congregation, so Mr. Jackson believes Grady shouldn't call on them."

Lydia laid her fork on her plate and stared at Angeline. "Why, that's absurd. I've a good mind to tell Harlie Jackson what I think of his underhanded tactics."

Angeline held up her hand. "Don't, Lydia. He already thinks you're too flamboyant and that you've brought loose women to town. Knowing I was pregnant when I arrived only confirmed that to him."

Near tears, Angeline said, "Grady would have been better off if we'd never met and married."

ANGELINE

"My dear, how can you say that? Grady is so happy now. His face beams when he looks at you and Matthew adores you."

As if to prove her point, Matthew banged his thumb and came running to Angeline. "Angel, kiss hurt." He held up his hand.

She lifted him and kissed his thumb, his hand, and under his chin. Then, she tickled his stomach. He giggled and hugged her neck. After a loud kiss on his cheek, she set him on the floor. Happy again, he picked up his toy and went back to playing.

Laughing, Lydia stood. "What an adorable mother and child you make. How can you doubt you've improved his life or Grady's?"

Her mentor's words soothed Angeline. She knew Matthew was a cheerful boy who depended on her. "We'll see what Grady thinks when confronted with whatever Mr. Jackson has planned. I doubt my name will be kept from the complaint."

After her friend left, Angeline worried as she went about her daily routine. Would Grady think he would have been better had she never come to Tarnation? She thought he would be safer, but she was so happy when he and Matthew and she were together.

When Grady returned late that afternoon, he had an envelope in his hand. He sat at the kitchen table and held the missive.

She set a glass of milk in front of him. "You can't absorb the words that way, Grady. You have to open the envelope and read the letter."

He met her gaze. "This is from the denomination office." His troubled expression conveyed his apprehension.

"But the church is non-denominational. How can that be?"

"I was ordained and hired through the church office in Indiana. And that's who sent this even though it originated in Fort Worth." As if he were handling something that might bite, he gingerly opened the envelope and pulled out a sheet of paper.

She watched as he scanned the letter. "What does it say?"

His knuckles were white as he gripped the sheet of paper. "I'm being investigated due to complaints against my conduct unbecoming a Christian minister. An official is arriving on Tuesday to conduct an interview and look into claims."

"All the way from Indiana?"

"No, from an area office in Fort Worth, which is the administration agency closest to Tarnation." He crumpled the letter and stood to pace the kitchen. "I knew something like this was coming,

89

but I had no idea Jackson would contact denomination headquarters."

"That awful man! Lydia came this morning to warn us of rumors she'd heard. I told her you and Matthew would be better off if we'd never met and I meant it. Marrying me was the last straw for those two dreadful men." Fighting tears, she laid her arms on the table and rested her head on them.

Strong hands clasped her shoulders. Gently, Grady pulled her to her feet and into his solid embrace. "Here now, don't think that for even a minute. Both of us depend on you. You really are the angel Matthew calls you. I know you were sent to rescue us."

She slid her arms around him and nestled her head on his muscular chest. His heart beat strong and steady and his powerful arms reassured her. "You're kind to say so. Matthew would have been as happy with any of the girls from Lydia's. I know you'd have been better off. Marrying you was selfish of me."

He nuzzled her hair and held her close. "No more of that talk. I wouldn't have asked you to marry me if I hadn't been sincere. None of the other young women caught my fancy. Angeline, I never gave much credence to destiny before, but I'm convinced you and I were meant to be together. We'll get through this pothole in our road."

She shuddered a sigh and stepped out of his arms. He always knew how to cheer her. If only he would say he loved her, she'd be the happiest of women. No, she should count her blessings instead of wishing for more.

She swiped at her tears and forced a smile. "I'll get your supper on the table. You must be hungry after your long day."

He released her but patted her shoulder. "See, if you weren't here, I'd have come home to a lonely house to eat alone. I love Matthew, but he's not the best conversationalist I've ever known."

She grinned. "He's the strong, silent type."

Chapter Twelve

On Monday, Angeline helped Grady and Mrs. Querado clean the church even more thoroughly than normal. They shined windows inside and out and polished pews and the floor. Hymnals and fans were neatly stowed in the designated holders on the back of the pews.

By Tuesday, Angeline had the house spotless. Just before time for the stage's arrival, she changed into her gray foulard dress and made certain Matthew was clean and in a cheerful mood from his nap. She gathered flowers from the beds she'd revived in front of the parsonage and set them in vases in the parlor and kitchen. If this man from Fort Worth was disposed to be judgmental, she certainly didn't intend to provide room for criticism other than her obvious pregnancy. She couldn't hide that from anyone.

When Grady escorted Reverend Harold Rhea to their home, she was relieved to see him smile. The visitor was average height and slightly chubby. His thinning hair was dark peppered with gray and he wore spectacles.

Entertaining important guests was something she'd learned at her mother's knee. She smiled and extended her hand. "I'm pleased to meet you, Reverend Rhea. Won't you come into the parlor and sit down?" She gestured to the kitchen where her son played with his toys. "That scamp is our son, Matthew."

The visitor looked puzzled. "I was given to understand Matthew was Mr. McIntyre's from a first marriage."

His statement shook her but she concealed her surprise. "That's true, but I love him as much as if I were his mother instead of only his stepmother. Since he doesn't remember otherwise, I'm the constant female figure in his life."

Grady smiled at her. "And she's wonderful with him. Matthew calls her his Angel, and I believe that's correct. The two males in this household are indeed fortunate to have my wife caring for us."

Frowning, Revered Rhea pulled some papers from his pocket. "I'd like to discuss the serious points raised in this correspondence."

Though her stomach roiled with anxiety, Angeline forced a smile. "If you gentlemen will excuse me, I'll bring in coffee and cake. You will stay for supper, won't you, Mr. Rhea?"

His frown didn't completely disappear. "Well, I hadn't planned to but now that you've asked, I'd be pleased to join you for a meal."

Angeline left the room but strained to hear what was discussed. She couldn't make out what the two men said. She added the coffee pot, cups, cutlery, napkins, and small plates of cake to a tray and took it into the parlor. They ceased talking as soon as she walked in the room. After setting the refreshments on a small table, she served each man.

Matthew came in and tugged on her skirt. "Angel, cake for me?"

Lifting him, she balanced him on her hip. "Of course we have cake for you. Let's go to your special big boy chair so you can have milk too."

While Matthew ate his snack, she started supper. She heard the two men go outside and wondered where they were headed. When she peered out the window, she spotted them walking toward the church. They appeared to be conversing amiably.

Her nerves were apt to send her screaming to her room if she didn't get herself under control. Grady would defend her as well as himself but what if he lost his job? If the church office removed him from this church, would he be removed from the ministry? What a crime that would be. She didn't know if ministers could be un-ordained.

***

Grady's knuckles were white where he gripped the arm of his chair. "I'd believe I deserve to know the charges leveled against me."

Reverend Rhea unfolded several pages. "Your accuser has quite a list that goes back several years. I realize this man is a malcontent, but some of the events cited require an explanation."

He exhaled and fought for calm. "I'm ready to defend myself."

The visitor extracted a pencil from his pocket. "Let's just go down the list. You hold a church service in the saloon?"

"The women who work there believe they wouldn't be welcome in the regular service and they may be right. I've invited them, but they prefer my coming there."

"And what does the owner think of this?"

"Usually, he serves as elder to help with communion but he also attends the regular service. The bartender and janitor attend the saloon service as do some of the others from around town. We hold the meeting at eight, well before the regular church service. Actually, I use the same sermon for both services."

Reverend Rhea checked an item on the list. "I see. All right, what about…your sermons. The letter writer says they're just cheerful talks rather than sermons on the Bible. How do you answer that?"

"I'm compelled to preach the New Testament as our Lord Jesus spoke. The accuser, who I'm sure is Mr. Harlie Jackson, is a fan of fire and brimstone preaching that strikes fear in the hearts of the listeners. I don't believe that's what Jesus taught, for he said he brought a new covenant."

The visitor checked another item. "That's true. Perhaps if we went to the church, you'd give me one of your sermons so I can learn what is usual."

Grady stood, somewhat reassured. "Good idea. Right this way."

They walked side by side to the church. Grady talked about the community and what he viewed as his mission there.

Inside the sanctuary, he pointed out how the services were organized. His insides trembled and his legs threatened to dissolve. Taking the lectern, he launched into his sermon from the past Sunday. Repeating familiar actions and words served to strengthen him.

As he went through the customary routine, he calmed. Even with only one person in the pews, the familiarity of preaching strengthened his resolve. When he'd finished, he gave a benediction and then walked toward Mr. Rhea.

The older man stood. "That was as fine a sermon as I've ever heard."

"Thank you. What you just heard is the one I preached last Sunday, but it's typical."

His brow furrowed with what appeared deep thought, Reverend Rhea led the way back to the parsonage. "And you say that's a typical sermon?"

"Yes. I change the scriptures each week and use them to teach the congregation and empower them to go out and live the message all week."

"And mid week services, are they much as on Sunday?"

"No, there's a much smaller attendance because only people in town attend on Wednesday. The elderly don't attend because it's dark when services end and they fear falling. Instead of a sermon, we have a Bible study. We go through the New Testament, but refer back to the Old Testament for background."

"I see. And where are you now?"

He couldn't prevent a grimace. "We're closing in on Revelation. I always dread that book, but we won't skip it."

Reverend Rhea tugged at his chin. "A difficult part to understand, especially to those who don't take history into account."

"Sir, I do what I believe the Bible and my training compel me to do. I won't apologize for doing what is right." He opened the door to his home, wondering how much longer he'd be allowed to live here.

The other minister smiled. "That's a lovely aroma. If supper is as delicious as the smell promises, you're a lucky man, Grady."

***

Angeline had prepared fried chicken, creamed potatoes, green beans, squash, corn, cucumber pickles, gravy, and a peach cobbler. She planned to serve coffee for the men and milk for her and Matthew. Checking the table setting once more, she was grateful for the linens and other fineries Grady's first wife had brought to the marriage.

When the men returned, she called them to supper. She gestured to the chair at the opposite end of the table from Matthew. They didn't need their son splattering food on their important guest.

Reverend Rhea took his seat. "My, you set an attractive table, Mrs. McIntyre, and the food smells delicious."

"Thank you. I hope you'll enjoy the meal." She allowed Grady to seat her.

As he did so, he said, "Angeline is a fine cook, as you'll soon see."

After his blessing, they dug into their food.

She served Matthew with potatoes, a drumstick, and green beans. With a bit of mess, he could use a spoon and fork. He held the drumstick in his hands. She kept the milk out of his reach until he asked for it or she thought he needed to have a drink.

Grady smiled at her before he addressed their guest, "Angeline makes fried chicken once a week because it's my favorite meal. As you can see, Matthew enjoys it too."

Reverend Rhea chuckled. "Guess all boys love fried chicken and that includes us grown boys, too. And this is cooked perfectly, Mrs. McIntyre."

The meal proceeded with conversation about the town and the congregation, but she could tell Grady was upset. She doubted Reverend Rhea discerned that fact, but she'd come to know the signs. He rubbed at his jaw or tugged his right earlobe when worried.

After the official had gone to his hotel, Grady closed the door and leaned against the wood as if he could barely stand. "I thought he'd never leave. Wasn't sure I could be pleasant much longer."

She took his arm and led him toward a chair. "Please tell me what's upset you this much."

He sat back down at the table so she poured him another cup of coffee.

Grady ran his hand through his hair. "I got a glimpse of the letter. Harlie and Ulys have written terrible things to the denomination office. I could lose not only this job, but be ousted as a minister if those accusations are proven."

"How could they be? Other than marrying me, you've done nothing wrong." She laid her hand on his shoulder. "I've never seen you in this much distress. I'm sure when Reverend Rhea talks to others in Tarnation, he'll hear only good things about you."

"Not if Harlie and Ulys have persuaded others to go along with them. They've been visiting around town recruiting troublemakers to join them."

"They won't find many, Grady. People here admire and respect you."

He didn't even glance up. "At the Wednesday evening service, Reverend Rhea is going to discuss the charges and hear comments from those in attendance to make his decision."

"But that's unfair. None of the elderly come to that service because they don't go out at night. And people from out in the county only come on Sunday mornings. That leaves out so many of the people who would speak up for you."

He appeared desolate. "I'm afraid we may be moving, my dear. I might have to start a church in a town that doesn't yet have one."

She reached over to clasp his hand. "I'll go anywhere with you, but don't give up yet. You of all people should have faith."

A slight smile tugged at the corners of his mouth. "You're right. I'm properly chastised." He pushed back from the table and stood. "I'll go work on what I'm going to say Wednesday night when I introduce Reverend Rhea."

***

Wednesday afternoon, Angeline peeked into Grady's office. "Matthew is asleep so I'm going to run a few errands. I won't be long."

He looked up from his desk, his spectacles riding on his nose. "I could go for you."

"Thank you, but I'll enjoy the fresh air and seeing people." She set her hat carefully on her head then grabbed her shopping basket.

Making her way first to the mercantile, she conferred with Josephine and Michael Buchanan. "The older residents aren't able to attend at night. I'm afraid Mr. Jackson and Mr. McGinnis will succeed in getting Grady fired." She couldn't contain her tears.

Josephine placed an arm around her shoulders. "Come in the back and we'll work on a solution."

After allowing herself to be led to the table in the storeroom, Angeline sank onto a chair. "I'm sorry. I'm so weepy lately. Mrs. Eppes said my moodiness is caused by being with child."

"Having your good husband's job threatened for spite is enough to make any woman cry. But we'll work something out. What if Michael rented a buggy and picked up several of the older people? I know they're afraid of falling if they walk after dark, but he could help them in and out of the carriage and walk them to and from their door."

Angeline dabbed at her wet cheeks. A glimmer of hope pierced her dark mood. "That would be a lot of bother for him. Do you think he'd mind?"

"I'm sure he won't, but I'll talk to him. He has a high opinion of Grady as a minister and both of you are our friends."

Encouraged by her friend's support, Angeline said, "He can only bring a few, though. I wonder if Adam would do the same with Lydia's carriage?"

"I'll ask him. He and Michael can divide up the older and infirm members of the church and try to get them to the service tonight." She tilted her head. "That sounds like Adam now. Wait here while I talk to the two men."

Angeline twisted her handkerchief, her muscles taut with

worry. She wondered if being so upset would endanger her child. Surely most women had problems during the nine months of their pregnancy.

Poor Grady. He worked so hard to minister not only to those who attended church, but all those in the community. In her opinion, he was an example of what a minister should be. How could two hateful men think otherwise?

The sheriff poked his head and shoulders through the curtain. "We're all set, Angeline. Don't worry about a thing."

Relief whooshed from her in a sigh. "Thank you. Your support means more than I can convey."

Adam waved his hand as if dismissing her concern. "All for a good cause. Michael and I will handle this problem. Don't think about it anymore. You take care of yourself and your family."

She stood and looked in the mirror over the small sink. After dampening her handkerchief in cool water, she smoothed the linen over her puffy eyes. She adjusted her hat and went into the front portion of the store.

She addressed Josephine and Michael, "Thank you both for your friendship. I thought I could count on your support for Grady."

She left and stopped by the butcher's. "Good morning, Mr. Horowitz. What looks best today?"

"Ach, Mrs. McIntyre, I have heard about the meeting tonight." A fierce look appeared on his face. "Aleida and I will be in attendance. We will not let your fine husband face trouble alone."

Because he was Jewish, he wasn't a congregation member. "Thank you, Mr. Horowitz. You and your wife are very kind. Grady and I appreciate your support."

He gestured to the glass counter. "As for my meat, I have a particularly good roast from one of Samuel Drummond's uncooperative herd members." He held up a chunk of beef.

"I'll take it. Grady will enjoy the treat. You know I serve stew often."

"Ja, and the fried chicken he loves." The butcher wrapped the meat in paper and tied the package with string. "You are a good wife to him and a good mother to his son. My wife and I have noticed how much happier the pastor is since your marriage."

A blush's heat spread across her face and pleasant sensations danced through her. "You're kind to say so. Thank you."

When she left the butcher's shop, Angeline exchanged greetings with everyone she met. She saw Reverend Rhea across the street talking to Adam in front of the sheriff's office. With a lighter heart, she walked home.

Home. The word sent warmth rippling through her. She had a home with a kind and caring man and a darling boy. Soon they'd have another addition. They might have to move, but for now they shared a cozy house which she loved.

True, it wasn't the mansion her parents owned. But there was laughter and happiness where she and Grady lived. No pretension, no manipulation, no harshness. She enjoyed her life now and looked forward to the future instead of dreading things to come.

Change raced toward her. She knew Grady wanted relations between them, even with her ever expanding waistline. Having his arms around her reassured and comforted her. He'd never force her, but how much longer could she deny his husband's rights?

She spent so much time with Matthew now. How would the little boy react to sharing her with a baby? A month before she was due, she'd begin preparing him for a baby. Did anyone else do that? She remembered her neighbors' difficulty when their new baby arrived and their son's jealousy threatened their peace.

Pausing at the parsonage's front walk by the flowers she'd tended, she turned and surveyed her surroundings. Already she'd come to love this small, dusty town—in spite of Mr. Jackson and Mr. McGinnis. Although she wouldn't be surprised to learn people had plenty to say in private, no one openly shunned her for her condition. Instead, people she met appeared smiling and welcoming.

With a sigh, she turned and went inside.

Chapter Thirteen

By evening, panic firmly gripped Angeline. She walked to the church sanctuary with her husband. He was deep in thought and silent. Dressed in his best suit with a fresh shirt, he carried Matthew. Reverend Rhea waited at the front of the church and they entered together.

The official gave no hint of what he thought or what he'd learned. She took her customary place on the second pew near the center aisle. She always rose and walked out with Grady to greet people at the door as they exited. The official sat on the pew directly in front of her and beside Grady.

Judging by the sound, a few people entered and took their seats. She recognized Harlie Jackson's gruff voice, which this evening held a hint of triumph. He spoke unintelligible words to someone else followed by a laugh. Heaven forgive her, she wished she could slap the man.

She heard the chatter of voices as people entered. Matthew waved at someone.

Mrs. Ramirez sat beside Angeline, and leaned near. "Large attendance tonight."

Surprised, Angeline pretended to attend to Matthew and glanced over her shoulder. The sanctuary was filling.

Grady rose and turned to face the congregation. Surprise showed on his face. "Thank... thank you all for coming. Seeing so many of you present is a blessing."

He cleared his throat as if overcome by emotion. "We won't have out usual Bible study tonight. Perhaps you've heard that certain members of the congregation have complained to the church office through which I was ordained and hired for this church. Reverend Harold Rhea is not making accusations but is here to address those complaints submitted. I know you will be honest and courteous to

Reverend Rhea as he completes his assessment."

Grady sat down and Reverend Rhea stood. He adjusted his glasses and pulled a few papers from his coat pocket. Unfolding them slowly, he laid them on the lectern and looked at those assembled. "A number of allegations have been made against Reverend Grady McIntyre. Although I've formed my preliminary opinion, I am obligated to read each charge and ask for your reaction."

"Number one, he consorts with saloon women and prostitutes on the Lord's day. Would anyone care to speak to this?"

Elias Kendrick stood. "I'd like to address that accusation. It's true that our pastor comes to the saloon at eight o'clock each Sunday morning to hold services for the people who work in the saloon and those who feel… unworthy and unwelcome in the regular service, and that includes the women who work there. I resent anyone calling these women prostitutes because they wear enticing dresses and serve drinks as well as sing and dance. They are not, to my knowledge, prostitutes. Rather than leave these people without the comfort and guidance of a church, Reverend McIntyre chooses to do the job he was called to do and minister to these people. How can anything be wrong with him serving all who need his message?" He took his seat.

Harlie jumped to his feet. "Those people don't contribute to the church so those of us who pay his salary are being cheated."

Elias rose again, his face red as he gazed at Harlie. "Ah, but they do contribute, each as he or she is able. I bring that collection to the church each Sunday. Would you condemn a man or woman because he or she can give only a little? Have you not read the value of the widow's mite, Mr. Jackson?" He returned to the pew and crossed his arms.

Reverend Rhea said, "I believe that concern has been resolved. Let us move on to the next item."

For an hour, the list went on with the same result. People in the congregation rebutted each accusation while Harlie and Ulys defended their claim. Many stood and spoke of the aid Grady had given and the kindness he'd extended in times of need. Angeline didn't know how much longer she could stand this. Thankfully, Matthew had fallen asleep on the pew.

Apparently, Reverend Rhea was as weary as she was. "I'll address the final item. After that I'll give my opinion and this matter will be closed. This concerns Mrs. McIntyre." He smiled sympathetically. "Would you care to leave, Mrs. McIntyre?"

She straightened her shoulders. "Thank you, but I will listen to the charges."

"I hesitate to use the language in the letter, but it concerns the fact that Reverend McIntyre married a single woman who was pregnant."

Grady leaped to his feet and whipped around to glare at Harlie and Ulys. "I will not allow my wife to be defamed. She is a kind and loving woman."

Angeline rose and raised her chin as she faced the congregation. "It's true that I was unmarried and with child when I came here. In fact Lydia Harrison rescued me when I had no place to go. You see, my father thought he had arranged a fine fiancé for me. The man forced himself on me and I refused to see him again. When I learned I carried his child, I told him. He responded by saying he would never marry a woman who wasn't a virgin and promptly left for Europe.

"My father refused to blame the man." She looked directly at Harlie and Ulys. "Like the two men who made all these trumped up charges, he blamed me and made me leave home with only the few belongings I could carry and twenty dollars. I ask you, how long do you think that would last? If Lydia hadn't taken me in regardless of my condition, my child and I would more than likely be dead by now." She turned at sat down, trembling with anger and embarrassment.

Murmurs rippled through the congregation.

Riley stood and told of her inspiring his patients to take their medicine.

Mrs. McAdams raised her hand. "I'm one of those she encouraged to follow Dr. Gaston's orders. Land sakes, a sweeter young woman never lived. And it's not because she married our fine minister. No, from the time she came to town she visited me and cheered me."

Mrs. Eppes said, "The first time I met her she carried my purchase home from the mercantile and then made me tea. She reads to me since I can't see well enough any longer. I so enjoy her company."

Angeline was crying with happiness as each of the elderly she'd visited spoke on her behalf.

Michael Buchanan stood. "Seems to me these two are perfectly matched. They both love serving others. They make a perfect couple and they both love Matthew."

Reverend Rhea held up his hands. "Time grows late and I've heard all I need to make my decision. I have heard you folks here tonight. I walked around the town and spoke with some of you. I listened to one of Reverend McIntyre's sermons. I'd say you folks are lucky to have this man as your pastor and his lovely wife beside him."

Cheers and applause broke out.

He looked at Harlie and Ulys. "After this ends tonight, I'd like to speak privately to the two men who penned this letter."

Grady rose and gave the benediction. Angeline picked up Matthew and walked out beside her husband. As people filed out, Grady thanked each of them for coming.

When everyone had left but Reverend Rhea, Harlie, and Ulys, the other minister waved. "Go on home and I'll close up for you."

"Thank you, Reverend Rhea." Grady took Matthew from her.

As they left the sanctuary, Angeline hugged her husband's arm. Her feet were light as air and she could have sailed over the housetops. "You won, Grady, you won! Your position here is safe."

He held her hand to guide her over the flat rocks that passed for a walkway. "For now. Who knows how this will end? Reverend Rhea still has to give his official statement. I suppose he'll do that in the morning before he leaves town."

"But he already said you're a good minister and the town is lucky to have you. Everyone cheered for you. The atmosphere was like a political rally or a… a theater performance."

"Theater is a good comparison. Harlie and Ulys love drama with them at the center. At the same time, they play politics like the most aggressive candidate for office."

"I don't understand what they hope to gain. They must be such unhappy people. I've never seen either of them or their wives smile. I don't like them but I can't help feeling sorry for them."

"Because of your considerate nature. I'm sure I have you to thank for our attendance. I don't know how you accomplished getting so many people to come tonight, but I'm grateful."

"Actually, Michael and Adam were the ones who drove buggies to pick up the elderly. The rest was you, Grady. People in this town admire and respect you. Even the Horowitzs were here and they're Jewish. Two complainers out of all those in this community are such a small percentage of your flock."

"A loud, clamoring percentage who enjoy spreading discontent." He opened the parsonage door and let her go in first.

She lit a lantern as he set Matthew on the floor.

Angeline looked at her husband. "I'd sure like to know what Reverend Rhea is saying to those two men, wouldn't you?"

He hung his jacket over the back of a chair. "I can imagine, but I doubt he'll be able to make a difference in their attitude. They don't believe they're wrong and nothing and no one will change their minds, especially not Harlie Jackson's."

Angeline put a tired and sleepy Matthew to bed. Before she went to her own room, she had something to say to Grady.

He sat on the parlor sofa, jacket off and tie loosened. Staring at the wall, he appeared deep in thought. Seeing him so desolate broke her heart.

After lighting the lamp, she sat beside him. She picked clasped his hand in both of hers. "Thank you for defending me in front of everyone. You have no idea how much that means to me."

He met her gaze. "I only spoke the truth, my dear."

"All my life my parents viewed me as an accessory to enhance their social standing. I had to behave a certain way, sparkle when we had guests, do anything possible to assist my father's social status. No one ever valued me for myself or defended me. Even when Horace assaulted me, my father blamed me. You're the first person who publicly spoke out in my defense."

He tugged her closer. "Angeline, I'm filled with compassion for you and with resentment toward your parents. They were cruel to use you and then turn you out instead of protecting you. But, I'm glad you came to Tarnation. Otherwise, I'd never have been blessed by having you as my wife."

"Thank you for saying so. I am blessed to have found you and Matthew." She wanted to tell him she was ready to be his wife in every way, but there was a knock.

Grady went to answer and found Reverend Rhea. "Come in. Have a seat."

The official did, hat in his hands. "I saw your lights on or I wouldn't have bothered you. I want to assure you that my report to Indiana will be glowing. I gave those two a stern talking to and I hope they'll take what I said to heart."

"I doubt they'll ever change, but I appreciate your effort."

"I've seldom encountered two more cynical and sanctimonious men." Reverend Rhea scrubbed a hand across his face. "Forgive me. I shouldn't say those things, but they really raised my anger."

Angeline asked, "Would you care for a dish of peach cobbler?"

The ministerial official perked up. "I'd be grateful. Probably get rid of the bitter taste those two left in my mouth."

She hurriedly prepared coffee and dished up the cobbler. She carried in a tray for the men. "If you'll excuse me, I'll leave you two to discuss matters privately and I'll turn in."

Grady's lovely hazel eyes held concern. "Are you all right, my dear?"

She offered him a smile. "Just a little tired from the week's events. Good night, gentlemen."

Fatigue dragged at her. Pregnancy combined with worry for her husband had her keyed up for the past few days. Now that the furor was over, her energy evaporated. Tomorrow night would be soon enough to tell Grady she was ready for intimacy.

Chapter Fourteen

The McIntyres were eating breakfast the next morning when Riley Gaston stopped by.

Angeline admitted him to their home. "You look exhausted. I'll bet you haven't had breakfast, have you?"

"Guilty on both counts." He followed her to the kitchen.

"Sit down and I'll soon remedy the breakfast part." She quickly scrambled two eggs while bacon fried.

Grady reached for another biscuit. "I'm happy to see you, Riley, but I suspect you came with bad news."

"Victoria Hunter fell during the night. Must've become disoriented and fell down the stairs."

Angeline set a plate of food in front of the doctor. "Mrs. Hunter? How badly is she hurt?"

Riley picked up his fork and dug into the eggs. "She'll be in bed for several days. Twisted her ankle and will be off her feet. Has a black eye and pretty good concussion plus bruised her arm and shoulder and sore muscles."

Grady laid down his knife. "What time was this?"

The doctor spoke around a mouthful of biscuit. "Around one. Judge heard her yell and started looking for her. Found her at the bottom of their stairway. He panicked and tried to lift her and hurt his back. She sent him for me."

Grady took a sip of coffee. "I'll go by this morning."

Angeline hurried to the ice box to see what she could prepare quickly. "I can send some of the roast we had last night."

Riley said, "They have a cook-housekeeper, Angeline. Save the meat for your family. Any little thing will cheer her. Why not make a bouquet of your flowers?"

"Oh, those will be faster, too." She grabbed her sheers and basket and rushed outside.

Grady waited until his wife was outside to speak frankly with his doctor friend. "I have to thank you for speaking up for me last night. I worried I'd lose my job, maybe even my license." He leaned back and stretched. "I love living in Tarnation and I'd like this as a permanent home. However, I was most concerned about Angeline."

Riley pushed his empty plate aside and leaned his arms on the table. "In your place, I would be too. You're both good for this community and I'd sure like for you to stay. What did that official say to Harlie and Ulys after we left?"

With a shrug, he replied, "I don't know. He asked to be left alone with them. He came by later and told me he hoped the two wouldn't be a problem any longer."

Riley leaned back and raised his eyebrows. "Harumph. Do you believe that?"

Grady laughed. "Not until I see results. But I don't care. If their constant bellyaching doesn't cause unrest among others in the congregation, then I'll be content."

"You're a better man than I am. I'd want them to grovel in public."

After picking up the coffeepot, Grady refilled both their cups. "Really, can you see either Harlie or Ulys ever apologizing?"

Riley took a sip of his brew. "Not in this lifetime. At least they were chastised for causing you so much trouble. Ought to slow them down for a few months. How's your wife feeling?"

"Seems to be doing well. She does tire more easily, but I guess that's normal."

"At this stage, yes. I'm glad you sent her to see me. She knew nothing at all about her condition or what to expect later. I asked her to return once a month until the last month when she should come in once a week."

"She's led a cold, loveless life. I intend to see she has warmth and happiness now."

"You can use the same, my friend. Your last couple of years haven't exactly been all fine and dandy." He stood to leave. "Thanks for the breakfast. You're a lucky man."

"Yes, I am. Have you chosen one of the Bride Brigade yet?"

The doctor stroked his mustache. "I haven't spoken for her, but I have my mind set on one I've taken a shine to. She doesn't seem averse to me so far."

Grady met his friend's gaze. "Don't wait too long, Riley. You're a fine looking man but you have a lot of competition."

After Riley left, Grady cleared the table. Before he could wash the dishes, Angeline returned with a basket of flowers.

His wife sent him a wide smile. "Thanks for your help, but I'll arrange these while you get dressed to go out. Mrs. Hunter must be aching something awful."

"Riley probably gave her laudanum or something to ease her. I'll hurry." He went to the bedroom for his tie and jacket.

When he went back into the kitchen, she had found a vase and created an attractive arrangement of mixed flowers. "Looks very nice. I'll stop by for the mail on my way back."

She widened her eyes. "I hope all we get is good news from now on."

He brushed his lips across hers and gave Matthew a pat on the head. His son was still eating bits of buttered biscuit and wore most of the bread.

Carrying the flowers, he walked the two blocks to the Hunter home. Mrs. Parnell, the housekeeper, answered the door. Inside he found the Judge slumped in one chair and Mrs. Hunter in another with her feet propped on an ottoman. Both had blankets covering them.

"I thought you'd both be asleep. How are you feeling?"

Victoria Hunter flicked her hand. "I've been better. Are those flowers from your wife's garden?"

Grady couldn't help smiling as he set the vase near her. "Yes, technically it's the church parsonage garden. She just revitalized it until it's flourished."

Mrs. Hunter lifted the flowers to her face and inhaled. "Lovely fragrances from a lovely woman. She's perfect for a minister's wife. I'm so glad you two found one another."

"Thank you, Mrs. Hunter. I'm thankful Angeline came into my life." He met the Judge's gaze. "How are you, Judge?"

"Feeling my age. Good thing Mrs. Parnell lives on the premises and came to our rescue." He sat a little straighter in his chair. "Say, I've a mind to tell Jackson and McGinnis you're going to sue them for harassment and slander if they don't stop complaining."

Grady chuckled. "You know I'd never do that, Judge."

"But telling them off will make me feel a lot better." He reached for a glass on the table beside him and took a sip before he smiled. "Don't worry, preacher. I won't cause you more trouble."

After another five minutes, Grady said a prayer for their quick healing and left. He never stayed long on calls unless the person he was visiting indicated they needed to talk longer. He only wanted to bring comfort and console, not tire the person he visited.

He went by the mercantile to check on his mail. Michael and Josephine greeted him.

He extended his hand to Michael. "Thank you both for helping me last night. I owe you more than I can ever repay."

Michael shook hands. "You owe us nothing. Friendship works both ways. Besides, you're a good minister and we want you to stay here in Tarnation."

Josephine handed him two letters. "You have mail today, one for you and one for Angeline."

Grady studied the envelopes. "This is from my mother. I don't know about the other. Looks fat, doesn't it? I'll go on home and give it to my wife."

As he walked toward home, his heart was bursting with gratitude. To a newcomer, the dusty street and drab businesses might not look impressive, but he knew the people in those stores and homes. At home, he had a lovely wife and growing son waiting for him and soon they'd have another addition to their family. He was one lucky man.

He walked into the kitchen and sat at the table. Matthew was in his high chair eating an apple. Angeline was busy shaping bread into loaves to rise.

He opened his envelope. "We have letters. This is from my mom. I'll read it to you."

"Dear Grady,

We were so happy to learn you've married and are happy. I wish we could have been at the wedding. I'm sure it was lovely.

Your Angeline sounds like the angel Matthew has named her. We were surprised she's with child, but who better than a minister to marry her? You two sound evenly yoked in work in the community. We are eager to meet Angeline and welcome her to the family.

We look forward to more details in your next letter. Yes, that is a hint. I know you are busy, but we want long letters telling us of your life there. Is the town growing or are the potential brides the only newcomers? How many of the young women have found a husband?

ANGELINE

Your father is doing well as am I. Jenny and Bob will welcome a new addition around the new year. Annie and Jim may adopt a child. David and Eleanor will be moving and we hope they will not go far. His company wants him to relocate either to Cincinnati or St. Louis. Having one son halfway across the country is hard enough.

We plan to visit you in October to help with the new baby if that fits with your plans. We hope you and Angeline and Matthew are well.

All our love,
Mother"

When he looked up, Angeline stood as if frozen with her gray eyes widened.

She wiped the remains of dough from her hands. "You told your parents about me? *All* about me? And yet they think we're well matched? They must be incredible people."

He smiled as he refolded the letter. "I think they are. I hope you don't mind that I revealed a bit about you and also hope you won't mind having them visit."

She sat at the table across from him. "I'll love meeting such kind-hearted people. No wonder you're such a good man with parents like yours. Have they visited you before?"

"Yes, twice. They came about five years ago and then when Matthew was born." He nodded at the other envelope. "Aren't you going to read your letter?"

She stared as if the paper might attack her. Tentatively, she reached for the missive. "From my mother. Who'd have thought we'd get letters from our mothers on the same day?"

She ripped open the envelope and read silently. Although she appeared angry, tears trailed down her cheeks. Throwing down the papers, she leapt up and hurried out of the room.

Unable to resist, Grady picked up the sheaf.

"Dear Angeline,

I have a great deal of news. Your father had a heart attack and died. His funeral was last week. The service was very well attended. Even the mayor and his wife came. We had luncheon here at the house afterward. Mrs. Culbertson catered. You remember what a nice job she does. Fontaine's did the flowers and the house looked lovely.

I met with the lawyers today for an eye-opening discussion. I had no idea we were as wealthy as we are. Your father invested well and I can live quite comfortably in my current lifestyle or better.

In addition, you have a trust fund left by your Grandmother Chandler in the amount of ten thousand dollars that was to be yours when you married. Although I shared your letter about your wedding with your father, he did nothing about the trust. I didn't know about it or I would have at least asked him to notify the lawyers. I've enclosed the information you'll need to claim your bequest.

Now that your father has passed on, you are free to come home. You can give your child up for adoption and leave that dusty little town behind. We can think of a story to tell our friends about your absence.

Love,

Mother

His heart hit his shoes. She had a huge inheritance. Would she leave him now? He couldn't let her go, not now. Tossing the papers on the table as he rose, he hurried after her. He found her leaning on his desk in his study.

He put his arms around her shoulders. "Angeline, don't go. I know you can go anywhere and do anything you wish now, but say you'll stay with me. With Matthew. We both love you."

She turned in his arms and laid her head on his chest. "I so wanted to hear you say that, Grady. I love you both. I would never leave you. Never!"

"When you rushed out, I read the letter. I thought... I feared you were going to pack your things and go to Missouri."

Her luscious lips thinned into a thin line. "You read that letter and thought I would go back? That I would give away my baby, the baby you call ours? You should know me better than that, Grady McIntyre."

"I hoped I did, but that inheritance came out of the blue and I didn't know what to expect when you rushed out."

"I came in here to get paper and pencil. We have to decide how much to spend and how much to save. I was going to make lists."

He laughed and hugged her. "My wonderful Angeline. How like you to be practical and busy."

"Thank you. I do believe this is where I belong. Even with the shame of your marrying a fallen woman, we do fit together very well, don't we?"

Gently, he tipped her chin to meet his gaze. "Yes, and I hope soon you'll trust me enough to be my wife in every way."

"I do now, Grady. I'm afraid I've fallen in love with my husband."

A broad smile split his face. "That's wonderful, my dear, because I feel the same way. I love you, Angeline McIntyre."

"Truly?"

"Yes, I realized at that party where I asked you to become Matthew's nanny. Adam suggested Elias should court you and I wanted to punch our sheriff in the mouth. All the way home, I pondered over why I should care. By the time I reached the parsonage, I realized I didn't want anyone but me even escorting you somewhere."

She stood and tugged on his hand. "Let's put Matthew down for his nap and go to bed ourselves, husband. Although it isn't night, I believe it's time we shared the same room."

He stood and swept her into an embrace. "Past time."

After hurrying back for Matthew, he tucked their son into bed for his nap.

Grady joined her in the other bedroom and gathered her into his arms. "I want to teach you the difference between your bad experience and making love as a husband and wife should."

When he broke the embrace, he took her hand and led her toward their bed. "Come, my love, and let's begin the new phase of our lives."

"I told you I would follow you anywhere and I meant that with all my heart."

He slid his arm around her shoulders. "How about if instead of you following me, we go together like a team, a partnership, equals?"

She slid her arm around his waist. "Perfect."

And they walked together into their future.

Epilogue

Tarnation, Texas October 1873

Angeline scanned the sanctuary. "My goodness, I believe the whole town has turned out to attend today."

Beside her, her mother-in-law Antoinette McIntyre held the newest McIntyre. Grady's elegant mother had hazel eyes like his, but her hair was dark brown, with a few gray hairs. This was the baby's first outing since her birth a week ago and Angeline had dressed her all in pink.

Antoinette watched her son on the pew in front of her. "I'm so glad we came. You've done so much since we were here when Matthew was born."

On the other side of Matthew, Andrew McIntyre glanced over the boy's head. Except for Andrew's brown eyes, Angeline visualized Grady looking like his father twenty or thirty years from now.

Andrew said, "Sure enjoyed the new guest room. I don't know if I would have invested building two rooms on to a house that wasn't mine. You're a generous woman."

Angeline cuddled Matthew to her. "If we have to move, we will. We love this community, though, and hope to stay here all our lives."

From the pew in front of them, Grady stood and walked to the lectern. "Thank you all for coming to the first service with our new stained-glass window. Our thanks to Vadim Kozlov and Colin Gallagher for cutting away the wall and framing in the window perfectly."

He grinned at the two men, both seated a few rows back. "Special thanks that they didn't break the window."

Chuckles rippled across the sanctuary.

Grady continued, "This was a major job but I believe it adds a great deal to our church. My wife and I love this community. Angeline

ANGELINE

donated the window because she wanted to repay all the people who've welcomed her to Tarnation."

The window was fifteen feet high at the arch. The artisan who'd traveled from Fort Worth depicted the scene Angeline had sketched. The result was even nicer than she'd hoped.

A blue background depicted the sky and rays of sunlight from a corner burst of yellow radiated toward earth. Midway, a dove with wings spread in flight carried an olive branch. An empty cross in the lower center was surrounded by a whirl of colors across the spectrum from clear to deep purple. The effect was awe inspiring.

Antoinette whispered, "It's a beautiful window. You were so generous to donate this. You've added a great deal to the reverence of the building."

Angeline smiled at her mother-in-law. In just over a week she had come to love Grady's parents. They'd arrived the day before their baby was born. Antoinette had helped Riley deliver the baby girl then Antoinette had taken over cooking and cleaning.

Grady said, "You met my parents last week, and now I'd like to introduce the newest member of the congregation, our daughter Antoinette Lydia McIntyre. I imagine there will be a number of little girls in this town named after Lydia Harrison, so we chose to use that as our daughter's middle name. The first name, Antoinette, is after my mother. Matthew has dubbed his sister Netta, so we decided that's what we'll call her."

Midway of the pews, Harlie Jackson stood. "I'd like to say something, preacher."

She saw Grady's body tense, but he nodded at Harlie.

"I want to apologize to Mrs. McIntyre—the young one who's your wife—and to you for criticizing and causing trouble. This isn't easy to say, but I was wrong. The new window and the additions to the church parsonage are good. Thank you for visiting my wife when she was sick. That's all I have to say." He clamped his mouth and sat on the pew.

Dead silence fell on the congregation.

Angeline couldn't believe her ears. She thought the day Harlie apologized would never come. He was too set in his ways and disapproved of everything she and Grady did. At least, that's what she had thought.

Grady's body appeared to relax. "Thank you, Harlie. A public

113

apology takes a strong man. Now, let us open our worship service with a prayer."

Light from the window cast an aura-like radiance around Grady. Angeline thought about how fitting that was. He'd saved her from shame and loneliness. Even more, he loved her and her baby.

After the prayer, he met her gaze with love overflowing from his eyes. How had she won the love of this wonderful man? Her heart was home. A real home with a man she loved and who returned that emotion.

She pondered all of this in her heart. All her dreams had come true. When she'd told that to Grady early this morning, he'd kissed her and said, "My Angel, the best is yet to come."

Dear Reader,

Thank you for choosing to read my book out of the millions available. If you'd like to know about my new releases, contests, giveaways, and other events, please sign up for my reader group at www.carolineclemmons.com. New subscribers receive a *Free* historical western titled *Happy Is The Bride*.

Join me and other readers at **Caroline's Cuties**, a Facebook group at https://www.facebook.com/groups/277082053015947/ for special excerpts, exchanging ideas, contests, giveaways, and talking to people about books.

If you enjoyed this story, please leave a review wherever you purchased the book. You'll be helping me and prospective readers and I'll appreciate your effort.

Caroline

If you downloaded this book without purchase from a pirating site, please read it with the author's compliments. If you enjoy it, please consider purchasing a legal copy to support the author in writing further books. If you can't afford to buy it, please leave a review on Amazon or Goodreads – it really helps!

Those who prefer reading western historical romance will enjoy being a member of the **Pioneer Hearts Facebook Group**. There you'll be able to converse with authors and readers about books, contests, new releases, and a myriad of other subjects involving western historical romance. Sign up at https://www.facebook.com/groups/pioneerhearts/

Read Caroline's western historical titles:

Mistletoe Mistake, sweet Christmas story set in Montana

Blessing, Widows of Wildcat Ridge, set in Utah, sweet
Garnet, Widows of Wildcat Ridge, coming January 2019

Loving A Rancher Series (sweet)
Amanda's Rancher, No. 1
The Rancher and the Shepherdess, No. 2
Murdoch's Bride, No. 3
Bride's Adventure, No. 4
Snare His Heart, No. 5
Capture Her Heart, No. 6
Loving A Rancher, No. 7

Patience, Bride of Washington, American Mail-Order Brides Series #42, sweet

Bride Brigade Series: sweet, set in Texas
Josephine, Bride Brigade book 1
Angeline, Bride Brigade book 2
Cassandra, Bride Brigade book 3
Ophelia, Bride Brigade book 4
Rachel, Bride Brigade book 5
Lorraine, Bride Brigade book 6
Prudence, Bride Brigade book 7

The Surprise Brides: Jamie, sensual, released simultaneously with three other of The Surprise Brides books which are: *Gideon* by Cynthia Woolf, *Caleb* by Callie Hutton, and *Ethan* by Sylvia McDaniel, each book is about one of the Fraser brothers of Angel Springs, Colorado

The Kincaid Series: Sensual, set in Texas
The Most Unsuitable Wife, Kincaids book one
The Most Unsuitable Husband, Kincaids book two
The Most Unsuitable Courtship, Kincaids book three
Gabe Kincaid, Kincaids book four

Stone Mountain (Texas) Series:

Brazos Bride, Men of Stone Mountain Texas book one, sensual
Buy the Audiobook here
High Stakes Bride, Men of Stone Mountain Texas book two, sensual
Buy the Audiobook here
Bluebonnet Bride, Men of Stone Mountain Texas book three, sensual
Tabitha's Journey, a Stone Mountain Texas mail-order bride novella, sweet
Stone Mountain Reunion, a Stone Mountain Texas short story, sweet
Stone Mountain Christmas, a Stone Mountain Texas Christmas novella, sweet
Winter Bride, a Stone Mountain Texas romance, sweet

McClintocks: set in Texas
The Texan's Irish Bride, McClintocks book one, sensual
O'Neill's Texas Bride, McClintocks book two, sweet
McClintock's Reluctant Bride, McClintocks book three
Daniel McClintock, McClintocks book four, sweet

Save Your Heart For Me, a mildly sensual romance adventure novella set in Texas

Long Way Home, a sweet-ish Civil War adventure romance set in Georgia

Caroline's Texas Time Travels
Out Of The Blue, 1845 Irish lass comes forward to today Texas, sensual
Texas Lightning, sweet, 1896 woman rancher comes forward to today
Texas Rainbow, sweet, 1920s flapper comes forward to today
Texas Storm, sweet, WWII WASP comes forward to today

Contemporary Western Hearts Facebook Group
If you prefer contemporary western romance, you'll enjoy interacting with kindred souls and authors by becoming a member of Contemporary Western Hearts Facebook Group at

https://www.facebook.com/search/top/?q=contemporary%20western%20hearts

Caroline's Contemporary Titles

Angel For Christmas, sweet Christmas tale of second chances, sweet

Texas Caprock Tales:
Be My Guest, mildly sensual with mystery, sensual
Grant Me The Moon, sweet with mystery,

Snowfires, sensual, set in Texas

Home Sweet Texas Home, Texas Home book one, sweet

Caroline's Mysteries: (Texas)
Almost Home, a Link Dixon mystery
Death In The Garden, a Heather Cameron cozy mystery

Take Advantage of Bargain Boxed Sets:
Mail-Order Tangle: Linked books: Mail-Order Promise by Caroline Clemmons and Mail-Order Ruckus by Jacquie Rogers, set in Texas and Idaho
Under A Mulberry Moon, nine-author anthology, July 2018, available for a limited time, novellas by Zina Abbott, Patricia Pacjac Carroll, Caroline Clemmons, Carra Copelin, Keta Diablo, P. A. Estelle, Cissie Patterson, Charlene Raddon, and Jacquie Rogers.
The Kincaids, Books 1-4 in one set, sensual, Texas
Cinderella Treasure Trove, excerpts, blurbs, author bios, and recipes from authors who write books with a new take on a fairy tale. Free
Musings and Medleys, blurbs, excerpts, recipes, and author bios from the authors in Under A Mulberry Moon. Free

About Caroline Clemmons

Through a crazy twist of fate, Caroline Clemmons was *not* born on a Texas ranch. To make up for this tragic error, she writes about handsome cowboys, feisty ranch women, and scheming villains in a small office her family calls her pink cave. She and her Hero live in North Central Texas cowboy country where they ride herd on their rescued cats and dogs. The books she creates there have made her an Amazon bestselling author and won several awards. Find her on her **blog**, **website**, **Facebook**, **Twitter**, **Goodreads**, **Google+**, and **Pinterest**.

Click on her **Amazon Author Page** for a complete list of her books and follow her there.

Follow her on **BookBub.**

Subscribe to Caroline's newsletter to receive a FREE novella of HAPPY IS THE BRIDE, a humorous historical wedding disaster that ends happily—but you knew it would, didn't you?

She loves to hear from readers at **caroline@carolineclemmons.com**

Made in the USA
Columbia, SC
07 October 2022

68647365R00065